AMONG
THE STARS

May·Bird
AMONG THE STARS

BOOK TWO

Jodi Lynn Anderson

SCHOLASTIC INC.
New York Toronto London Auckland Sydney
Mexico City New Delhi Hong Kong Buenos Aires

No part of this publication may be reproduced, stored in a retrieval system, or transmitted in any form or by any means, electronic, mechanical, photocopying, recording, or otherwise, without written permission of the publisher. For information regarding permission, write to Atheneum Books for Young Readers, an imprint of Simon & Schuster Children's Publishing Division, 1230 Avenue of the Americas, New York, NY 10020.

ISBN-13: 978-0-545-04183-6
ISBN-10: 0-545-04183-X

12 11 10 9 8 7 6 5 4 3 2   9 10 11 12/0
Printed in the U.S.A.   40

First Scholastic printing, September 2007

Map on pp. x–xi by Peter Ferguson
Images on pp. 102 and 137 by Sammy Yuen Jr.
Book design by Christopher Grassi
The text for this book is set in Berkeley Old Style.

For a few of my girl heroes: Amanda Clair, Emma McClintic,
Emily Jo-An, and Katherine Mary

CONTENTS

Acknowledgments

I would like to acknowledge Rosemary Ellen Guiley and her book *The Encyclopedia of Ghosts and Spirits* for providing such extensive information on the folklore of spirits, spooks, and specters. I also wish to acknowledge Professor Verlyn Fleiger for introducing me to North Farm and its mysterious mistress.

In addition to the usual suspects, I would like to thank Bertrand Comet-Barthe for his many kindnesses. I would also like to thank my niece Amanda Anderson VanDerSluys for being my first young editor. Her encouragement has been much cherished.

Finally, I want to acknowledge *all* of my nieces for inspiring any part of May Ellen Bird that is worthy, and special, and true.

EDGE OF THE WORLD
NORTH FARM
CARNIVAL AT THE END OF THE WORLD
PETRIFIED PASS
RISK FALLS
WILD HUNT
STYX STREAMWAY
N
TRAIN TRACKS

Ever After
hing Platte
Platte of Despair and Unknown Lands
The Colony of the Undead
Everville
Hideous Highlands
Hocus Pocus
Ether
South Place
Southern Territories
Bogey
Catacomb Cliffs
Belle Morte
Dead Sea

Prologue

rees are not supposed to have favorites. But they had always been slightly partial to May Bird.

Over the ten years since she'd been born, the woods of Briery Swamp, West Virginia, had peered through May's window night after night. They had watched over her thoughtful brown eyes, the imaginative crook of her head, the strong character of her knobby knees. The trees had laughed at the jokes May told to her cat. Their leaves had whispered over her wild inventions, her colorful stories, her drawings.

But since May had been missing, the trees had watched over her mom instead.

Ellen Bird was like and unlike her daughter. They both had the same thoughtful eyes and the same dark hair, the same sweet, quiet ways. But while May had always run wild through the trees in her sparkly black bathing suit, sticking feathers she found behind her ears and tucking flowers into the pockets of her shorts, Ellen had always liked to sit and work. Now, she only sat . . . and waited.

The day May and her cat had gone missing, the police had

rolled up to the house like an overturned bushel of apples, crisscrossing the rambling white walls of White Moss Manor with red and blue lights. May's classmates had followed shortly after with cards and cakes and flashlights, whispering phrases of regret to one another:

Maribeth Stuller: "I teased her for wearing black rubber boots on Mondays."

Claire Arneson: "I never traded my fruit squishes for her peanut butter balls."

Finny Elway: "I laughed at her for playing badminton with her cat."

The truth was, none of them had been very nice to May Bird.

For weeks the residents of Hog Wallow, Little Yellow Church, and Droop Mountain had combed the woods in the fine-tooth way. But when they had called May's name, only the crickets and the trees had talked back.

And so, but for a forbidding and vast stretch of briars that simply couldn't be crossed, they had covered Briery Swamp and turned up nothing but bad cases of poison ivy.

Ellen Bird had remained on the porch wrapped in an old quilt and a new sorrow.

And the woods, unable to speak in words she could hear, kept their secrets—about the night May had wandered into the trees in the dark, about the strange glow that had taken her away, and about the lake, where a glowing figure swam night after night, waiting for the next person who might wander her way.

A person who might come looking beyond the briars. A person, perhaps, like a sad, brown-eyed mother, searching for her girl.

Part One

Across the Hideous Highlands

Chapter One

The World's Largest Demon Toenail and Other Wonders

On a train hurtling past a black sea, on a star far above the earth, a hairless cat lifted his nose to the air, sniffed, and let out a tiny howl. Even Somber Kitty didn't know why he did it. Instincts were weird that way.

He stared across train car 178 and let out a frustrated sigh. May, sitting at one of the car's windows, appeared to be lost in her own thoughts. Somber Kitty let his chin sink down onto his paws again.

May gently twirled the pendant Pumpkin had given her in the City of Ether—one half of a tiny silver coffin that, when placed with its other half, showed the engraving: NEVER TO BE DEARLY DEPARTED. She hardly blinked as she stared at the sight that had appeared on the horizon a few moments before.

Far above the vast, dark, oily Dead Sea that, May knew, held even darker things beneath its surface, dark clouds swirled. Strokes of lightning occasionally threaded their way across the sky, seeming to tie it in crooked bows. It looked like the world's worst thunderstorm was going on somewhere across the sea. Despite the distance, the sight fell over May's heart like a shadow.

May shivered and reached for Somber Kitty. Only too happy to oblige, the hairless cat—who was considered very cute by some, very ugly by many others—leaped into her lap, placed a paw on each of her shoulders, and licked her cheek with his sandpapery pink tongue. May scrunched up her face in disgust, but she smiled.

As she and Kitty peered out the window together, she thought of her mom, and the many strange and mysterious things that had happened to her since she had fallen into the lake in the West Virginia woods and come out on the wrong side of life, into the world of ghosts. The train slowly veered west, pulling away from the dark, glistening seashore, back into the Hideous Highlands, blanketed in dusk. In the Ever After, it was always dusk and the stars zipped through the sky as if they were meteors.

Decrepit old billboards—like the ones they'd been seeing for the last few days—zoomed past:

WORLD'S LARGEST DEMON TOENAIL, NEXT EXIT

PETEY'S PIRANHA SHACK: OUR PRICES CAN'T BE BEATEN,
EVEN IF YOU'VE BEEN EATEN

THE HAIR STILL THERE SALON: DREAD LOCKS,
SHRUNKEN HEAD MASSAGES,
SCALP REATTACHMENT AVAILABLE
(DISCOUNT FOR THE FIRST 100 HOMESTEADERS TO MENTION THIS AD!)

They'd already passed the World's Largest Tombstone, the World's Longest String of Ectoplasm, several billboards promising a good time at the Poltergeist Corral, and several more announcing something called "The Carnival at the Edge of the World."

Sighing, May stood and moved forward through the opulent but decayed train car. In the first cabin she came to, Captain Fabbio's long, ghostly frame sprawled across two beds pushed together, neatly tucked under the sheets and snoring under his mustache.

Beatrice, in the cabin beyond, lay with one dainty, transparent arm splayed over a pile of books, the top of which was *Baedeker's Most Popular Destinations for Typhoid Victims*. May took the books, carefully marked their open pages, and put them on the bedside table, then quietly slid a pillow under her friend. Kitty, dangling rather close to Bea's face as May did this, touched her spectral cheek gently with his paw, then pulled back gingerly and licked his paw pads to warm them up.

May took his paw in her hand and blew on it warmly. Bea, like most spirits, was always so cold.

In the next cabin—the one that May, Somber Kitty, and Pumpkin shared—Pumpkin lay curled up around his blanket, snoring. Kitty did not even attempt to pat *Pumpkin's* cheek. He simply leaped from May's arms onto the top bunk. But every time a snore issued from the sleeping ghost's rather large, pumpkin-shaped head, he gazed down at him, then lifted his nose in the air and looked away.

At Pumpkin's request for her to "make it special," May had decorated the cabin like a royal Persian boudoir, scavenging moldy bolts of silk, shiny bells, star lights, and other decorations from various parts of the great train, deserted but for its skeleton conductor, who neither spoke nor reacted when May and her companions popped up to the front of the train to see him. Once the boudoir had been completed, Pumpkin had insisted on being called "Your Highness" whenever anyone in the room addressed him.

"Meow?" Somber Kitty whispered.

"All asleep," May said, misinterpreting Somber Kitty's question. What he had really meant was, *Are you sure you don't get the sense that someone we love is in danger?*

At the moment May didn't sense anything. In fact, she was perfectly content. She had almost forgotten, just then, that she was stranded in the Afterlife, on a star a million miles from home. Friends, she had realized, could make you do that. Forget the things that worried you most. May had only just learned this; before the Ever After, her only friends had been cats.

It had been seven days since these very friends had helped her escape a fearsome creature called the Bogey at the City of Ether. Since then May had planned twenty-seven escape routes from the train in case it was stopped by their enemies. She had installed booby traps at the caboose of the train, as well as in the dining car—involving string, empty slurpy soda cans, and some ectoplasm she'd found in the bathroom. She had even made scarecrows of herself, Pumpkin, Kitty, and the others to use in case of an emergency, though she didn't know how they would actually help. For less urgent reasons, she had also invented a mustache curler for Captain Fabbio, who liked to look dashing while he was on the run, and fashioned a clip to hold book pages down for Beatrice as she read.

For whatever reason, the Bogey was leaving May and her friends alone. He had to know exactly where they were. He had seen them leap onto the train. And it was a nonstop train straight to the north edge of the realm. May wondered if the Bogey had died when he'd been trampled by all those Egyptians outside Ether, but Bea had patiently reminded her that he had been dead in the first place.

May peered out her window into the distance again, as if she might see the object of these fears climbing up the sides of the train at any moment. Up ahead, the mountains of the Far North were visible, but just barely—tiny points rising from the horizon and shrouded in a haze. The Hideous Highlands stretched endlessly between them—a vast wasteland of ancient roadside curiosities.

Once, Bea had explained, the northern train route had been wildly popular among spirits all over the realm and had been populated with all manner of frontier towns and attractions. But for the past couple of hundred years it had declined to the point of extinction, until almost every train was empty and most of the attractions had shut down, fallen apart, and begun to disintegrate.

May sighed, then climbed onto the bunk beside Kitty to make her bed—but she quickly shrank back.

A large manila envelope floated just an inch above the mattress, addressed:

May Ellen Bird
Car 178
The North Train
The Ever After

May looked around, hopped down off her bunk, checked the outside hallway, left and right, then climbed back onto the bed and gazed at Somber Kitty.

He blinked at her drowsily, his eyes green, lazy slits. If he had seen anyone deliver the strange package, he wasn't talking.

May touched the corner of the envelope with her pinky, pulled it toward herself, and turned it over.

She gasped. The stamp on the back was familiar. With her pinky, she traced the insignia of leaves shrouding a mysterious face. The only distinct feature visible was a pair of eyes, and they stared out at May with a look that was both inviting and sly—enticing and, perhaps, dangerous. It was the same stamp that had been on the letter she'd received back in Briery Swamp, inviting her to the lake. The stamp of the Lady of North Farm.

After a moment's consideration May tugged the envelope open. A blinding light flew into her face and made her throw her hands in front of her eyes, shutting them tight. On the back of her eyelids, to her shock, these words were scrawled in bright white letters:

> Dear Miss Bird,
>
> Congratulations on your narrow escape from the Bogey! The Lady is smiling on you—but then, the Lady's smile can be very ambiguous.
>
> We look forward to your arrival. The Lady has something she wants to ask of you. We understand that you have something to ask of her, too. In case you are wondering, she has it in her power to grant whatever you wish.

May's heart skipped along a little faster. She thought imme-diately of home—its shaggy green lawn and the wayward line of White Moss Manor's roof, the sagging porch, the shady woods. Wouldn't those things be a welcome sight? She pictured herself running up the stairs, through the front door, into the arms of her mom.

> *We're sending you two freshly baked northern cookies and two bottles of grade A North Farm milk. They'll keep you from getting hungry or thirsty as long as you stay in the Ever After. You and your cat will need to consume them quickly. Please do not beat around the bush.*

May blinked her eyes open and looked into the pouch. She pulled out the cookies and milk, examining them in wonder, and laid them on her bed. When she shut her eyes again, more words appeared.

> *Please hurry up. The Ever After is unraveling faster than an old sweater. Your enemies are not as close as you think, but they are closer than they should be. Speaking of which, you are about to hit a bump in the road. Good luck with that.*
> *Never forget that the way back is forward.*
> *Sincerely,*
> *H. Kari Threadgoode*
> *Secretary*
> *P.S. The Lady wants me to say hello to Somber Kitty. Apparently, they go way back. Of course, being a cat—and a living cat at that—puts him in much danger.*

The letters on the backs of her eyelids flickered out. When May opened her eyes, the envelope, too, was gone. She looked at Kitty, then at the cookies and milk, then back at Kitty. All she could think to say was, "You go way back?"

"Meow," Somber Kitty said, sniffing one of the cookies, trying to change the subject. What he would have said, if he could speak English, was that everybody knew the Lady of North Farm, in some way or another—they just didn't *know* they knew. The Lady was, in fact, woven into the very fabric of the universe. You couldn't miss her.

But then, people were generally very foolish about these things. They didn't believe in the existence of ghosts, for instance. But then, even ghosts did not know that trees could laugh. So Somber Kitty guessed that the dead and the living were pretty even. Only cats came out ahead.

"It was a telep-a-gram. They have booths in all the major cities," Bea explained, running her fingers along her long blond curls to make sure each hair was in place. She folded her hands in her lap. "You think it, and then you send it. I've tried to send one to my mother," she said, frowning, "but you need to have an exact address."

Bea and the others, gathered in the dining car, had listened with concern as May shared the contents of her strange letter.

"A bump in the road?" Captain Fabbio twirled his mustache. "What means this?"

"I don't know." May brushed a crumb of cookie off of Somber Kitty's mouth. He'd eaten his right away, before May could catch him. She looked at her own cookie, then took a tiny nibble. If Somber Kitty was going to be poisoned, then so would she.

"I don't see why I don't get a cookie," Pumpkin muttered. He narrowed his eyes at Kitty, but that only made him look like he needed glasses. Somber Kitty licked the crumbs out of his whiskers extra loudly (for Pumpkin's benefit) and gazed out the window insouciantly.

Over the several days they'd spent on the train, the house ghost and the living cat had come to the realization that the other considered himself May's best friend. Since then they had regarded each other with cool disdain.

"This Lady, she no know what she is talking about," Fabbio blustered.

May shrugged. It seemed the Lady knew a whole lot more than May wished she did. She knew May was in the 178th car of the northbound train, for instance. She had known when May and Pumpkin were in the Catacomb Cliffs by the Dead Sea. She had known the woods of Briery Swamp.

Bea's forehead wrinkled with concern. "I'm sorry, May, but I don't like the sound of it. 'The Lady's smile is ambiguous' and all that. . . ."

May crossed her arms. There was no question that the Lady was questionable.

"But she says she'll grant me what I desire," May murmured. It was the one line of the telep-a-gram that stood out like a flashing sign in her mind. More than the ambiguous smile or even the danger. What she desired, more than anything, was to see her mom again.

Bea reached across the table and patted her hand, making

May's skin tingle at the touch of her cold, ghostly fingers. She wore a look that was both encouraging and unutterably sad. Beatrice Heathcliff Longfellow had a permanent sadness about her that made its way even into her smiles.

"I know, May. But everything I can find on the Lady says she's surrounded by danger. Look here." Bea shuffled through the books—opened to various pages—strewn across the table in front of her and pointed to a passage.

Lady of North Farm
Location: The frigid wilds of the Far North.
Known for: Acts of great kindness, acts of similarly
tremendous nastiness, excellent sewing skills,
keeping trespassers captive for all eternity,
associating with beings of light.
Holo-photo: None. None of the holo-tographers
we sent ever came back.
If you're planning to visit: See page 195.

May turned to the page. It contained a list of insane asylums in the Greater Ether Area. She leaned back.

Bea closed the book and rested on it, arms crossed under her chin. She had read almost every book in the train library, some twice, looking for information that might lead her to her own mother, whom she hadn't seen since she'd died of typhoid in 1901, a few days behind her mother. She had been—and still was—eleven years old.

May noticed deep circles around Bea's eyes, and for the moment it seemed her ghostly glow had gone a little dim.

"Well, I don't think I have a choice," May ventured. "I did everything to avoid the Lady before. And look, here we are. On a train, headed straight for her. I don't think it's a coincidence."

They were just throttling past the neon-lit World's Most Rotten Hot Dog stand, but May was staring past it, thinking of the long journey that had brought her here: her failed attempt to find the way home without the Lady's help.

"No *choice*. No coincidence. Pah! We take this train on purpose." Fabbio waved his long arms dismissively. "And what about this *bump* in the road?" Fabbio looked out the window. "I see no bump."

Pumpkin let out a loud sigh. " 'Bump in the road' is an *expression*." He was wearing a toga he'd found in an abandoned suitcase, tied with a curtain tie. He flounced one tassel around dramatically as he talked, smiling haughtily at Kitty from the corner of his eye. "It doesn't mean a *real* bump. It means—"

Bump.

"Meay!"

Somber Kitty, hissing, bounced against one of the closed windows, then landed on all fours. Pumpkin flew across the table under a cascade of cards; Beatrice and May hurtled off of their bench onto the ground; Fabbio tumbled flat against the wall behind him.

Scccccccccccccccrrrrrrrrrrrrrrrrrrrrccccccccccccccccchhhhhhhhhhhhh hhhhhhhhhhhhhhhhhhhhhhhhhhhhhhhhhhhhhhhhhhhhhhhhhhhhhhhhhh!

The train came to a dead halt.

A bone-chilling stillness followed.

The Bogey.

Pumpkin whimpered and zipped under the table. Somber Kitty positioned himself between May and the rear car door. And they all readied themselves for whatever might come through it.

Chapter Two

Cleevilville #135

Curled in the corner of the car, they all waited to see what would happen next.

Several minutes passed. Finally, crouching, May reached for her death shroud, which lay on a seat nearby. As she slipped into the robelike garment, tying it around her neck, it became transparent, and her body—black bathing suit, shorts, and all—took on the ghostly, translucent tinge of a ghost. She remained just a pinch more colorful than the others, and she didn't levitate—but at least she blended.

"Meow," Somber Kitty whispered, shimmying toward the windows like a soldier. Clearly, the curiosity was killing him.

"No, Kitty." May crawled forward and pulled him back by the scruff of the neck. Cats—in fact, animals in general—had been banished from the Ever After long ago, because the Bogey's Blach Shuck dogs were scared of them. Living people had been banished too. In her shroud May was safe. But Somber Kitty wasn't.

"Sit," she whispered sternly. Somber Kitty lay down, restless as a tiger. May inched her face up to the glass.

Outside, crooked rooftops rose above a high stone wall.

"It's a town," she whispered. She pressed her nose against the glass and looked down the side of the train in either direction. "There's nobody out there."

The others drifted to the glass and peered out. Somber Kitty leaped onto a chair and placed his paws against the windowpane.

A stone arch hung above an opening in the wall, just to the left, proclaiming the town to be Everville, T.E.A.:

PARDON OUR DUST! COMING SOON: CLEEVILVILLE #135. COMING ATTRACTIONS: CRAWL-MART, CHAR-BUCKS, SKULLBUSTER VIDEO.

"Crawl-Mart?" May whispered.

"They have all the shelves at floor level for spirits who have been de-limbed," Beatrice explained. "They're very popular."

Fabbio floated down the aisle and reappeared a moment later with his Fabbio scarecrow. In a flash he'd opened the window and shoved it out. It went flopping into the air and landed on the ground beside the train.

Everyone looked at him quizzically.

"To see if anybody comes to get me," he said.

Nobody did.

"Should we go outside?" May asked.

"Meay," Somber Kitty said definitively.

Bea backed away. "I don't know. Perhaps we should just stay here until the train starts moving again. I read in the *Star Gazer* about a specter in Hag Hollow who was taken by a gang of gremlins when she was waiting too long for her train. "

"There's no such thing as gremlins," said Pumpkin wisely,

smoothing back the small tuft of yellow hair that sat atop his giant, misshapen head. Still, his eyes darted to the windows nervously.

They waited. And waited. But the train didn't move.

Finally, as if by silent vote, and with Pumpkin trailing far behind, they all floated down the aisle toward the caboose.

The town of Everville was small, with crisscrossing streets that ran vertically from the train tracks. On either side were dwellings—spooky, colorful, and lopsided houses with drooping wooden balconies leaning over the avenue. Dangling signs hung like fall leaves over the street, advertising various businesses: Near D'well Saloon, Jake's Dry Goods for Drowned Specters, Sepulchral Salon and Day Spa. Filmy, glowing tumbleweeds blew up and down the roads.

It looked like an average ghost town, if May had had to guess what an average ghost town would look like. But something had gone *very wrong* in Everville.

The buildings were empty. The streets were completely deserted. The doors to every building hung open, as if every single soul had had to leave in a hurry. Things were strewn across the streets: cowboy hats, shackles, newspapers, books, toys. Two guns had been dropped in the street, about twenty paces away from each other, as if they'd been poised for a duel. A gaggle of hangman's nooses hung in the town square, swinging empty and forlorn, as if they had just been vacated.

And there was something more. A shadow hung overhead like a dark, wet sock. It was heavy and heartless. Unlike the rest of the Ever After, which glowed with an eerie green light,

Everville sat bathed in an *absence* of glow. May remembered the stormy skies she had seen from the train.

They kept walking. In the town square a giant plaque had been erected in front of the Everville town hall. In glowing, glinting, red letters it read REMEMBER, BO CLEEVIL IS WATCHING YOU. A pair of red glowing eyes lay emblazoned beneath the words. Pumpkin nibbled his nails and looked around at the empty buildings.

May walked up to it slowly, reaching out to touch the letters. Within an inch of their surface, her fingers began to tingle, and she yanked them away.

Few spirits had ever seen Evil Bo Cleevil, but according to all reports, he made the Bogey look like a cupcake. And over the years, he had gained power—buying up (and stealing) prime real estate, assembling a horde of ghouls and goblins to haul off innocent spirits to his fortress in the northeast, building an undersea lair called South Place. He was the one who had sent the Bogey to catch any living people, or Live Ones, hiding in the realm—and suck them into nothingness through his horrible fingers.

May wasn't sure that she wouldn't choose being turned into nothing over meeting the owner of those terrible eyes. But *The Book of the Dead* said she would meet him. *Would*, and then some.

"I hear Bo Cleevil is part vampire," Fabbio whispered fretfully.

"I've read that every time you hear a bell ring, Bo Cleevil has locked another spirit in his fortress dungeons," Bea said. She straightened the silky blue ribbon—a little frayed around the edges—that cinched the waist of her dress. "And he rides a giant bat."

May cast a fearful gaze at Beatrice. "Didn't he banish all the animals?"

Beatrice wrinkled her forehead. "He may have let a few favorites stick around. You never know."

"No, no, no," Pumpkin said. "Bo Cleevil is a hitchhiker who roams the roads of the Ever After looking for a ride."

Everyone was silent for a while, thinking their own thoughts. May was thinking of *The Book of the Dead* and its predictions. It made her heart go cold inside.

"The sign says it's Cleevilville number one thirty-five," Beatrice said finally. "Do you think this has happened to other towns, too?"

May's heart felt too heavy to say yes, but she *felt* yes. She picked up one of the books lying open on the ground, slipping her finger inside to hold the page, and turned it to look at the cover: *The Modern Ghoulish-to-English Conversational Dictionary*.

She read the page:

Page 28

Conversations you might have in a town you are about to destroy:

Kkkeooeoa jaaa?: *What are you up to?*

Kkkeeooeoa hghghfuslvblblll: *I am up to no good, as usual.*

Glklklkbjbjbjbullljjj ggggiiiyyylsdshio: *Let's go pillage that street.*

Jrglglgleehhee?: *Why the long face?*

Hjsdsjkji skjkjiojehvhvaijifd: *I am in a very bad mood, as usual.*

Lklklklkdsne euebhgbhb?: *Can you please tell me where the bathroom is?*

Hklklkle ghuhurel knsibbibbib: *I'll bet her guts are delicious.*

May's throat grew tight as she read on.

> Popopwoewn dshuhuihiuh: *Let's eat her.*
> Kllklklihhii glubbhur?: *What's that smell?*
> Hohfodhope. Skjkljkl lkjhhljklw, jurlll?: *It's my armpits.*
> *They smell fabulous, huh?*

Beatrice, too, had picked something from the debris: a charred newspaper. She opened it gingerly and flipped through the pages, her blue eyes moving back and forth rapidly. "Nothing about us anywhere. It's a good sign." She looked hopefully at May.

May scratched Somber Kitty's ears. "Can I take a look?" The front page was scrawled with the masthead *The Daily Boos*. There was a specter interest story about a group that was banding together to keep a favorite sepulcher from being turned into a nightclub. In local news a tele-token mint had been broken into, meaning some spirit was on the loose and able to teleport all over the realm, making many other spirits jealous. A neighborhood watch had formed in West Stabby Eye for three poltergeists who had escaped a nearby zoo.

"I speak poltergeist, you know," Pumpkin said.

"That's nice, Pumpkin," Beatrice said, taking the Ghoulish-to-English dictionary from May and tucking it into her bag.

"No, really, I do."

"I'm sure you do," May said politely.

"I still think they're spooky, though."

May grinned. She used to think that Pumpkin was pretty spooky himself. In fact, she had once thought he was the most terrifying creature she'd ever seen. Until she had gotten to know him.

"*I'll* say. They can make you lose your mind," Beatrice said matter-of-factly. "Just by yelling nonsense at you. I read it in my book on Dark Spirits. You have to cover your ears to keep from going insane. And also . . ." She considered, biting her bottom lip as she tried to recall. "Oh, yes, they smell like rotten bananas."

May continued flipping through the pages of the newspaper. There was an op-ed on the pros and cons of cannibalism, though one contributor complained the topic was irrelevant for everyone except certain groups of pygmies. A local man had found a talking skull in his nightshade bushes and was trying to find the body it belonged to.

Of their escape from Ether there was no evidence but for a small blurb on page 27 that read:

LIVING CAT/SACRED DEITY SPOTTED IN ETHER

Spirits in the City of Ether were shocked Tuesday when a living cat with exceptionally large ears and little to no fur was spotted near the Eternal Edifice. Local authorities attempted to capture the cat, who escaped into the desert on foot.

An unusually large number of Egyptian witnesses on the scene claimed that the cat was sacred and asked that he please be returned to the main pyramid on Tutankhamen Drive in New Egypt if found. New Egypt officials are offering a reward of one mummy of solid gold encrusted with rubies for the safe return of Dinè Akbar, or "Big Ears."

"Good thing John the Jibber's not with us," Pumpkin joked, but May turned a look of such hurt upon him that his smile vanished. "Sorry."

Judging by the way their former traveling companion, John the Jibber, had betrayed them at the Eternal Edifice, there was no doubt that he would have traded any one of them for a mummy in a heartbeat. Still, May shuddered at the memory of watching his soul disappear into the Bogey's horrible, sucking fingers.

Nonplussed, she continued to flip through the pages. "Nothing about us anywhere," she finally said. Page 6 had a box of movie listings at the Everville Spectroplex:

Guess What's Coming to Dinner?

Tomb with a View

Drifty Dancing

"I suppose they won't be showing any more movies in Everville," Beatrice said, and everyone was silent.

Pumpkin shivered. He took the paper from May's hands. "Does anyone want to hear their horoscope?" he asked. Without waiting for a response, Pumpkin asked everyone their birthdays and then read Bea's: "'Gemini. Be on the lookout. You are destined to meet a horrible fate.'" Fabbio's: "'Leo. You may as well stop being so pompous. You're headed for doom.'"

May told him Somber Kitty was an Aquarius. He scowled and sighed and said flatly, rolling his eyes, "'Aquarius. Trust your instincts. You are right to be sad.'"

"Meay," Somber Kitty said pensively. Somber Kitty was always sad.

Pumpkin looked at May.

"Sagittarius," she said warily.

Pumpkin scanned the page. "Ah." He stabbed the paper with his finger, then frowned. "'Stay in bed today.'"

Everyone looked at the ground, utterly depressed.

"What's yours, Pumpkin?" May asked.

"Oh." Pumpkin thrust his finger into his mouth and blushed. "I don't have one."

He looked so crestfallen, even Somber Kitty looked sympathetic. Unlike Bea and Fabbio, who were specters, Pumpkin was only a ghost. And that meant he had never been born.

"Is all superstition," Fabbio said stiffly, thrusting his chin in the air. After a moment he added with a sniff, "I am no pompous. I am the picture of modesty."

His eyes traveled to Beatrice, and then he dropped the rest of his words. She was twisting the long locks of her hair thoughtfully. "What are we going to do, May? Without a train? North Farm must be thousands of miles away."

"I don't know." May thought better of her reply and added, "But we'll figure it out."

"I'm sure if we just think it through . . . ," Bea added gently, still running her fingers through her curls. She looked at Captain Fabbio uncertainly.

On the long train ride Bea and Fabbio had shared tales of their many travels, including the day they'd found each other. Beatrice had happened upon him sitting in a cobblestone alley in Fiery Fork, newly deceased, crying into his collar over the loss of his men in the Alps.

Young Bea, who'd been dead for many long years by then, took him under her wing, revealing her own search for her mother and suggesting that they find their lost loved ones together. They had covered the entire southern half of the realm, from city to town to cemetery, before they'd encountered May and Pumpkin and landed on the train headed north.

"Well." Bea smoothed her skirt and tried to look reassuring. "You're our leader. I'm sure it'll come to you."

"I'm sure you're right," May said halfheartedly.

Back home May had always dreamed of being an Amazon princess, leading a brave group of warriors through the forest behind her house. Now she surveyed her loyal band: a foolish house ghost who jumped at the word "boo"; an Italian air force pilot with a bad sense of direction; a bookish girl specter; and a courageous but melancholy cat with no fur. And May, shortest of anyone except for Kitty, knobby kneed and bashful, was supposed to lead these four to an unknown farm, in an unknown land far to the north, to talk to an unknown Lady.

And this Lady, if they ever made it to her, would do one of two things: something extremely kind or something equally nasty.

Deep in the recesses of South Place, a holo-vision set cast a blue light along the walls of a small, dark room.

On the screen a blob of a ghost, wearing a moth-eaten suit, addressed the camera: "And in other celebrity news, this Wednesday several eyewitnesses saw the Ever After's most fearsome henchman, the Bogey, floating across the desert, flat as a pancake and without any pants. Many question whether this had anything to do with the mysterious occurrences at the Eternal Edifice on Tuesday. Others wonder, if the Bogey isn't wearing his pants, who is?"

One gleaming white eyeball watched the screen from the shadows, and its owner gave out a low, raspy growl. One flat arm, clad in a black sleeve, shot forward and clicked the channel button on the remote with its suction-cup-tipped fingers.

A letter lay on a nearby table, shining in the glow of the screen. The deadly fingers laid down the remote, and drummed on the paper. . . .

> B.—
>
> *Received your telep-a-gram explaining the strange news coming out of Ether. That a house ghost, three specters, and a living girl could find admittance to the Eternal Edifice gives me great pause. But since you swear to me you have made them into nothing, I will let you slide. A little girl and a house ghost are merely a joke. But take care that this kind of breach does not happen twice.*
>
> *Bogey, the time has arrived. You know what I mean. From now on, you will need to put all of your energy into preparing a meeting of every Dark Spirit in the realm. Let's shoot for October thirty-first. I will arrive at midnight.*
>
> *Sincerely,*
> *B. C.*

The holo-vision flickered.

"Do you sometimes feel lost, afraid, hopeless?"

In the shadows the white eye widened.

"Are you evil but not quite evil enough to get the job done? Do you need someone vicious enough to take care of your enemies but wily enough to keep it confidential? A hunter with a sly mind and killer instincts?"

The face moved forward into the light—long, white, flat, with sunken cheeks, a pointy chin, and razorlike white teeth—and nodded.

"Call Commander Berzerko!"

The face sank. The Bogey touched his empty eye socket ruefully. The missing eye had gotten stuck in the flip-flop of an Egyptian spirit and disappeared, never to be seen again by anyone except itself. He thought of his poor Black Shuck dogs whom—in a rash moment of anger—he'd banished to the Swamp of Swallowed Souls.

He wanted the girl destroyed. The girl *and* her friends. And it certainly had to to be kept secret.

But even the Bogey knew better than to unleash a spirit like Commander Berzerko. She had not been let out of her pen for over a hundred years . . . and that was probably best for everyone involved.

Still, the Bogey's white eyeball gleamed with a thought. There was another option.

He reached for the skull-o-phone.

For a moment he hesitated, his suction-cup-tipped fingers poised over the teeth. And then he began to tap the teeth with his fingers, dialing someone—a group of someones—who would surely take care of the girl.

He called the Wild Hunters.

• • •

That night May and the others camped far from the town, in case whoever had taken the residents of Everville returned. They used the classified section of the newspaper to build their fire. Because of this, they missed a few things that might have been of some interest to them.

They had not seen the ad for Fast-Forward Motion Potion, for example, nor had they scanned the lonely spirits listed in the personals section (*Is It You-hoooo? Lost Soul Seeking Same*). They also missed the announcement for the gathering of a group called STARD (Spirits Totally Against Realm Domination) at an undisclosed location due south of the Scrap Mountains. The truth was, May and her friends were too concerned with their immediate futures to notice.

Tomorrow, they decided after talking long into the night, they would head north—back into the emptiness of the Hideous Highlands.

Chapter Three

Something's Gone Bad at the Snack Shack

"Can you carry me?" Pumpkin asked.

May rolled her eyes at Pumpkin. "I'm already carrying Kitty." Pumpkin scowled.

Somber Kitty stirred in his papoose, which May had fashioned out of some curtains she'd pulled from the train. He peered over May's shoulder and waved his tail at Pumpkin contentedly.

After two days of traveling, they were still following the train tracks due north. As the telep-a-gram had promised, May had felt neither hungry nor thirsty.

"Look." Beatrice pointed to a circular building up ahead and to the left. It was the long-promised Poltergeist Corral. It looked like someone—or something—fierce had shattered a hole right through the front wall, which was enormously high and at least three feet thick. They stuck to the tracks, studying the corral curiously as they floated and walked by. It looked like it had been abandoned for a hundred years, but flashing signs still hung crookedly from the walls:

POLTERGEIST CORRAL
POLTERGEIST TRICKS!

THROW THINGS AT POLTERGEISTS
PET THE POLTERGEISTS!

Somber Kitty let out a low growl.

"Poor poltergeists," May said.

The captain made a loud clicking sound with his mouth. *"Poor poltergeists!* Pah! Horrible creatures."

They kept moving, and soon the corral was far behind them.

When they tired, the group camped alongside the deserted tracks, in the dusky shadow of a crumbling billboard advertising the Carnival at the Edge of the World. In the picture an enormous spiked black Ferris wheel soared above a park full of lights and attractions, countless specters and ghosts smiling at one another as they tried their luck at games or as their vaporous forms blew out of shape on the rides. The billboard was torn and peeling in many places but still displayed the words RIDE THE TUNNEL OF TERROR! VIEW THE KNOWN UNIVERSE!

For some reason, it reminded May of Lucius. All those spirits smiling and laughing made her think of the horrible fate he was probably enduring under the sea.

"Why so sad?" Captain Fabbio asked, staring hard at May. May squirmed. Out of her group of new travel mates, she felt the most shy with Fabbio.

"I was just thinking of someone. A boy."

"Ohhh, your *boyfriend*?" Fabbio oozed, raising his eyebrows and twirling his mustache knowingly.

"No. He was a boy I met in the Ever After, before I met you and Beatrice. A specter."

Captain Fabbio and Beatrice both looked at her expectantly.

"I sort of got him . . . sent to South Place."

"Ay, Dio mio!" Fabbio exclaimed.

Beatrice gasped.

"She didn't really *get* him sent there," Pumpkin said defensively, twirling the half of the NEVER TO BE DEARLY DEPARTED necklace he and May shared. "It just happened. He got hit by seawater."

May gave Pumpkin a grateful grimace of a smile.

Fabbio twirled his mustache and cocked an eyebrow at Beatrice. Anyone who touched a drop of seawater was sent immediately to South Place, the realm of Dark Spirits far under the sea. "I'm sure you didn't mean to," Beatrice offered to May. She looked to Captain Fabbio to confirm this.

"Eternal torment by ghouls and goblins eees . . . not so bad," Fabbio said. "Could be worse."

"How?" Pumpkin asked, biting his finger, curious.

Fabbio searched the sky above his head. "Errrrr . . ." Then he scowled and threw up his hands. "I will think of it later."

May tried to feel reassured, but later that night all her mistakes stuck to her mind like a briar on a pair of tights. If she had never talked Lucius into coming out of the Catacombs, where he'd been hidden safely for so long, he would have never been hit by seawater. And it made her wonder what other mistakes lay ahead.

She looked at her companions, all asleep but for Somber Kitty, who stared at her drowsily, purring softly and keeping watch. Kitty only blinked at her and whispered, "Meay." May didn't understand what he'd said, but it amounted to something like he believed in her—much more than she believed in herself. May tried to picture herself as the hero *The Book of the Dead* had described:

MAY ELLEN BIRD: *Known far and wide as the girl who destroyed Evil Bo Cleevil's reign of terror. Resides in Briery Swamp, West Virginia.*

But in her mind's eye, all she could see was the patchwork blanket on her bed back home. The crack on the inside wall of her closet that looked like a question mark. The gathering of four pine trees by the trail in the woods, where she used to lie on the pine needles, pretending it was the warrior queen's bed. She dared not think of her mom right then. It would have made the ache too big for such a small body. She thought only of these little things that she missed.

She reached out and stroked Somber Kitty. She recalled, proudly, his surprising victory against both the Bogey and his horrible dogs, the Black Shucks. If May knew one thing, it was that no danger, at that moment, would have surprised her.

Ellen Bird sat poised over the pile of laundry in May's closet, holding a pair of May's black overalls. Today was the day she had gotten up the courage to do her missing daughter's laundry.

What had made her pause were the tiny green bits embedded all over the overalls, from the knee to the ankle. Curious, she dug one out with her nail.

A briar.

Ellen rubbed the briar between her thumb and forefinger.

Abruptly, she stood and approached May's bedroom window, peering out at the tops of the trees.

She was thinking of a night May had come home from the woods, saying there had been something bad there. Ellen remembered the sight of May, curled up in her blankets like a caterpillar, her overalls discarded on the floor.

It had been her daughter's wild imagination. Hadn't it.

Ellen rubbed the briar a minute longer. And then, heaving a long-suffering breath, she dropped it into the wastebasket by the door and walked out.

"If she's not in the mountains, there are lots of other places my mother could be," Bea said hopefully, looking behind her to make sure May was there. They had gotten an early start that morning, but the mountains only teased them from the horizon, and it was hard to tell how much progress they'd actually made.

"She could be in one of the coastal towns or even in one of the cities. The Ever After is a big place." Her eyelashes fluttered thoughtfully. "Even if I *did* put up signs all over the City of Ether and send telep-a-grams to the Board of Spirits with Unsightly Diseases in all the major cities and stop at every typhoid sanitarium in the south . . ."

Beatrice had been looking for her mother for more than eighty years, and she had covered a lot of ground.

"But I do hope that she's in the mountains."

Beatrice had not stopped thinking out loud since they had left Cleevilville. Her mind wandered from all the strategies she had used to locate her mother to where she might have gone wrong or missed something and how she might fix it. "I'm sure she must be somewhere I haven't checked yet."

Pumpkin, not paying attention, hummed to himself happily as he drifted along up ahead, occasionally falling behind when he thought he saw something shiny or interesting, then zipping to take the lead once he ascertained it was nothing of interest after all.

Fabbio licked his thumb and thrust it in the air. "This good Italian trick to find how long we have to go," he said, holding his thumb against the wind. Then his shoulders slumped. "It is telling me there is long way to go."

"Isn't that a trick to find out if it's going to rain?" Beatrice asked.

Fabbio stiffened, as if realizing, with a start, that she was right. Then he swatted at an imaginary fly, pretending not to have heard her.

When Bea didn't fill in the silence, he cleared his throat and interjected a poem.

"The plains is like my lover's eye
She makes a good'a pizza pie."

"I didn't know you liked poetry, Captain," May said kindly.

"Yes." Fabbio stood erect. "What you are wondering is true. I was born with heart of poet. The genius words, they come from inside, I know not how. I no have girlfriend." He added with a wink, by way of explanation, "This about the lover is not a true story. All up here." He tapped his head.

"Astounding," Beatrice said. The girls grinned at each other as Fabbio cleared his throat and began another one, this time comparing the endlessness of the plains to the endlessness of his love for his dear uncle Bonino, who played the flute.

As he listened, Somber Kitty let out a low, pensive meow. He regretted at that moment that he understood more English than he spoke. May thought, as Fabbio finished his poem, that they may have discovered what was worse than being tormented by ghouls and goblins for all eternity.

By the end of the day there were more worrisome things on everyone's minds. The mountains didn't seem to be any closer, despite their long day of traveling.

"Maybe we should turn back," Beatrice said uncertainly. The highlands rolled along in every direction with no sign of change. "It's not too late to head back to Ether. At least we know how far back it is."

May considered this as she looked around at the empty, rolling landscape. She shoved her hand into her pocket and grasped the manila envelope. It seemed the Lady should be sending her some kind of signal of what to do. But there had been nothing.

They moved on in silence, each thinking their own thoughts. The mountains were specks in the distance. Or, from the mountains' perspective, May imagined, *she* was a speck in the distance. Her hope faltered inside her, realizing this.

"I made my room into Hawaii once," May said, trying to distract herself with warmer thoughts. "I made a lagoon and pasted paper trees on the walls. But the inflatable pool I was using for the lagoon popped, and it flooded the room. She got so mad!"

Beatrice smiled appreciatively at May's story. "I went to a

cotillion with a purple bow instead of the pink one that matched my dress. Mother was very displeased."

May grinned. "One time I slept with my Halloween candy, and it melted into my hair and Mom had to cut it." That was how she'd ended up with her short black bob. Before that, May's hair had been long and lustrous and down to her waist, like a wild forest child.

They recounted other times they'd made their moms angry. Like when May flushed her toothbrush down the toilet, pretending it was a submarine, and the old pipes burst. Like all the times she'd been sent outside dressed and combed and had returned with muddy quartz rocks gathered in her shirt, thinking they were as valuable as diamonds and hoping to spend them in Hog Wallow. Mrs. Bird had built a special shelf in May's room to keep them all safe.

It made them almost forget. It made them almost feel as if their moms were just behind them, catching up, and not impossibly far away.

NECROMANCY NANCY'S SNACK SHOPPE, a sign ahead announced. A shell of a house perched on the rocky hill beyond it, its doors all long fallen in and its frame sagging to the left. Shingles had slid off its sides and lay in piles at its base. Somber Kitty gave the air a thoughtful sniff from his papoose as they passed the sign and turned toward the shop.

"If I get home, I am going to behave better," May said, her eyes on the horizon ahead, where the faintest shadows of mountains formed.

"If I see my mother again," Bea mused, trying to pass the time, "I'm going to tat a lace handkerchief for her."

"If I see my men again, I never ever gonna let them go," Fabbio blurted out with emotion, then cleared his throat and tugged at the medals on his uniform self-consciously.

"Something smells terrible," May croaked, pinching her nose with her fingers.

Beatrice drifted to the front doorway and wrinkled her nose.

Pumpkin raised his nostrils to the air. *Sniff, sniff, sniff.* "Smells like bananas."

Whoosh!

May flinched just as a teapot flew past her head.

She stared after it as it went tumbling across the dirt. It had come out of one of the windows of Necromancy Nancy's.

"Oh no!" Beatrice said, casting a look at Fabbio. Pumpkin whimpered.

"Ay, Dio mio," Fabbio said, backing up, his eyes pinned to the shack. Somber Kitty leaped from his papoose and hissed at the empty, gaping doorway.

"What is it?"

"Shhh," Beatrice hissed, taking May by the strap of her bathing suit and yanking her backward. Pumpkin zipped backward too.

Bea's eyelashes fluttered wildly as she quickly scanned the area around them. "They're here," she whispered.

Fabbio grasped the hilt of his sword. "We are to being very still. They may be surrounding us."

"Who?" May turned to stare at Bea quizzically at the very same moment that a pie plate came shooting through the doorway, just missing her ear. Her hands flew to her face as a shrill cry rang in her ears.

And then they saw it. A *something* appeared in the doorway of the snack shack. It didn't have a shape, really—it was just a glowing, lopsided orb of hazy light. In its hazy arms it held a jumble of plates, bowls, and candlesticks.

"Bip bop diddum duddum waddum choo!"

A torrent of items came flying at them from the doors and windows of the house. A bottle of shampoo flew at May from behind. Just as she turned, somebody pinched the back of her neck, then her cheek.

"Cootchy cootchy!"

Next to May, Beatrice crouched to miss a teacup. "Run!"

"Bip bop diddum duddum waddum choo!"

Fabbio pulled out his sword and began waving it in the air wildly as they sprinted forward alongside the tracks, dodging the rocks butting out of the soil. Laughter and other sounds of delight followed behind them. So did silverware. A butter knife missed May's ear by half a centimeter. A fork grazed Fabbio right under his nose, combing his mustache.

"Gobble gobble gee, gobble gobble guy!"

"What's happening?" May asked, craning her neck to look behind her. She could just make out fuzzy, indistinct shapes—balls of mist and light zipping along behind them, occasionally oozing slime in long dribbles on the ground.

"Poltergeists!" Bea yelled, clutching the sides of her head. "Cover your ears!"

The group fled across the highlands, and the poltergeists followed—over small rises and rocks, down furrows in the land.

May, who'd already been ready to fall down from exhaustion,

felt her legs going wobbly beneath her, and she finally tumbled forward, thudding into the grass.

Fabbio came to a halt. Beatrice, Kitty in tow, slammed into his back with an "Ugh." Pumpkin zipped behind a rock.

May felt a pair of cold hands on her shoulders and a dribble of slime down her back. "Gobble gobble gobble gobble," it whispered.

"Sha na na na?" a voice said. The voice sounded familiar.

"Diggy diggy?" the poltergeist holding May's shoulder replied, releasing her.

"Well, gobble. Gobble gobble."

Everyone gazed in astonishment at Pumpkin. He and the poltergeists looked like they were having some kind of meeting.

Finally, Pumpkin looked back at May and the others, irritated. "Can we have some privacy, please?"

Bewildered, Fabbio, Beatrice, May, and Kitty walked about twenty yards away.

A few minutes later Pumpkin came floating over to them.

"They say they can help."

"Banna fanna fo fanna!!" the poltergeists called over Pumpkin's shoulder. Pumpkin slapped his hands on his knees and laughed.

"What did they say?" Beatrice asked.

"Nothing." Pumpkin cleared his throat, shooting a glance at Fabbio's curled mustache. "Just a joke."

"Okay. But what are they saying?" May was starting to get annoyed.

"I told them we're trying to get north. They said they'll carry us to paradise if we want. They said the spirits there are pretty brave; they might be able to help us get north."

Bea, Fabbio, and May looked at one another. They shrugged. Paradise didn't sound that bad.

"I don't know. Poltergeists are very unpredictable," Beatrice said.

"Hobble gobble."

"They say that's typical of specters, to be so rude. They say they're a misunderstood and oppressed species of spirit that has never gotten the respect it deserves."

"Gobble gobble."

"In fact," Pumpkin translated, "they have started the Union Against the Defamation of Poltergeists and suggest you could be held accountable for your comments."

Everyone stared, disbelieving.

"Zippety doo da."

"And they said, so what if they occasionally steal stuff and turn spirits mad and try to knock them out with heavy objects? That is their right as poltergeists," Pumpkin finished with his nose in the air.

Everyone looked to May for a decision.

"Why are they willing to help?" she asked suspiciously. "Why us?"

"Dippity do!"

Pumpkin paused. His wide, crooked mouth fell into a scowl. He looked at Somber Kitty, then sighed and muttered, "They say, because they like your cat."

May looked at Kitty, who licked his paw casually, then at the poltergeists. She looked to the mountains in the north.

"I don't know. . . ."

What if the poltergeists were liars, like John the Jibber had been?

But then, what other choices did they have?

"I think . . . I think out of all of our choices, it may be the least terrible one," May finally said, looking unsurely at the others, who nodded agreement.

With that, the poltergeists hoisted them all into the air and started carrying them west across the highlands.

Chapter Four

The Edge of Paradise

It was a couple of hours before the poltergeists stopped up ahead on the dusky horizon and began to gabble, leaping up and down. Their baggage, whom they let down now, looked over the rise and were greeted with an unexpected sight: a patch of scrubby, thin, glowing trees surrounded by a wide moat.

"Gabble gabble!"

Pumpkin waved. "Gobble!"

Without another gabble, the poltergeists zipped off, on to some other adventure.

Everyone looked at Pumpkin. "What?" he asked self-consciously.

"We just had no idea you could . . . do that. You said you could, but . . ." May trailed off.

Somber Kitty looked off into the distance and yawned, trying to appear bored. Pumpkin and May shared a smile that only they understood. It wasn't the first time Pumpkin had surprised her. He blushed.

They all approached the edge of the moat—which spanned by a narrow bridge—and tried to peer into the sparse scattering of trees on the other side. *Paradise.*

Fabbio cleared his throat. "I have a poem about this. It is called 'Across the Moat I'm Looking, to See What Is Cooking.' It is like this. . . ."

After they'd listened patiently to Fabbio's poem, which was a sonnet in iambic pentameter, May suggested they cross the moat, but very carefully. If the poltergeists could attack them so easily, maybe others could too, and maybe they wouldn't be so friendly. She fastened her death shroud extra tight. She didn't want anyone spotting her as a Live One and blowing their Bogey whistle, which would summon him lickety-split.

"Wait, what about Kitty?" Beatrice asked.

May looked down at her cat. There wasn't much use of *her* looking ghostly when *he* looked so very alive and, well, catlike. "You're right," she said with a sigh, embarrassed. She could be so forgetful sometimes.

"Kitty, you're going to have to hide here until we find out what kind of spirits are around," she said.

"Meay?" Kitty mewed softly and sadly, tilting his head to one side and giving May his best sad kitten eyes. But May shook her head.

"I'm sorry."

Somber Kitty sneezed reproachfully. Then he curled up under some nearby branches. "Mew," he said, with finality.

Everyone gave him a kiss on the top of the head as Pumpkin stood and watched, making jealous kissy faces behind their backs. Fabbio lingered, stroking Kitty's ears. "You stay safe, little Kitty."

Under Somber Kitty's watchful gaze, they each crossed

the moat, Pumpkin insisting on floating directly behind May. Then they disappeared into the trees.

The travelers made their way slowly through the grass. "Yow," May whispered. "Ow. Ouch! *Pumpkin!*" She turned around. Pumpkin stood centimeters behind her, biting his fingers.

"Can you *please* stop stepping on my heels?"

"Can I have a piggyback?"

"No," May hissed.

"Can I go back and wait with Somber Kitty?" he whispered.

"If you want."

"Will you take me?"

"No!" May, Fabbio, and Beatrice said in unison.

Pumpkin was silent for a few moments, then he whispered, "Can somebody hold my hand?"

May sighed, but she let Pumpkin slip his frigid fingers into hers.

A few minutes later they approached the last of the cluster of trees, obscuring what looked like a clearing. Fabbio stuck out his arm theatrically, and they all came to a halt. "On count of three, we pull back branches and look." Beatrice, however, had already pulled aside some branches. They leaned forward.

The sight was breathtaking. In the evening starlight lay a wide vale—a deep, sprawling valley of green grass that spread itself downward in a bowl toward huge, slate gray cliffs that climbed into the sky. And crashing along down the middle, breaking against the rocks in great puffs of white foam, was an enormous waterfall—glowing neon blue water rushing toward a large pool, where it crashed and foamed with deafening speed.

Waterslides, burrowed smoothly into the rock, wound down the cliffs on either side of the falls, curling toward the lagoon below. Tiny purple and yellow nightshade flowers floated on the grass like polka dots on a green dress, along with a giant trampoline and something that looked like a cannon.

Tree houses dotted the trees around the field, and several tents made with sheets and sticks were strewn across the lawn. A sweet breeze blew through the glowing grass. Ukulele music floated from some unknown spot, playing a sweet Hawaiian tune.

Fabbio wiped a tear of joy from his eye. Beatrice let out a long sigh. Pumpkin squeezed May's hand tighter. May felt a smile in her heart. Just looking at the beautiful water had a peaceful, soothing effect on her. "Paradise," she whispered.

Suddenly, from the left, a knot of spirits, their heads stuck with feathers, came barreling past the trees. Another group chased after them, shooting arrows and yelling wildly.

Some were missing heads or arms or legs. Others were bent and twisted into odd shapes. Besides the feathers they had tucked in their hair, they wore aviator suits, loincloths, swim trunks, camouflage. Never in the Ever After had May witnessed such a ragtag group of spirits.

As the travelers looked on, a figure bringing up the rear seemed to catch sight of them out of the corner of his eye. He skidded to a halt and aimed one of his arrows in their direction, peering at them through the trees.

"Nobody move," he said. A white line of sunblock ran the length of his nose, his green eyes sparkled wildly. He wore a pair of fluorescent orange shorts and an orchid-printed T-shirt.

He had a slight bluish tinge to his lips. After studying them a moment longer, he lowered his arrow and held a hand up in the air. "What's up, dudes?"

May looked at the others, then back in the direction in which they had left Somber Kitty. Pumpkin gave her a little shove forward.

"Um, hi."

The spirit thrust his hand toward May. "Name's Zero."

"I'm May Bird." May gulped, tightening her death shroud. "This is Beatrice Heathcliff Longfellow, Pumpkin, and Captain Fabbio."

Zero directed his widening smile at Beatrice. "Welcome to paradise." Then he seemed to recall something. His mouth lowered in a frown. He lifted his arrow again, aiming it at them.

"You're trespassing."

Chapter Five

Risk Falls

The travelers huddled together on a boulder in the middle of the grass, staring out at the hundred or so specters who had gathered to catch a glimpse of them. "Ohhh," Pumpkin moaned, cowering behind May. Beatrice gave him a look that urged him to be brave. The spirits were a fearsome group—mostly young, all mangled or maimed in some way. By the way they were dressed, May picked out snake charmers, race car drivers, mountaineers, parachutists. To the right, those not curious enough to join the gathering occasionally hurtled over the edge of the falls, screaming and plummeting with a crash into the lagoon. A few shot out of water cannons nearby.

Zero levitated above the boulder beside them, as if he were presenting them for show-and-tell. "Listen up, y'all," he bellowed. "I caught these spirits in the trees, spying on us."

"We weren't really spying on you," Beatrice offered helpfully. "We're trying to get north and—"

One of the spirits in the crowd waved his hands in the air. He was missing his lower half.

Zero pointed to him. "What's up?"

"Where's the pizza?"

"What pizza?" Zero asked, looking around hopefully.

"Dude, I thought they were delivering a pizza." The lower-halfless spirit and a few others muttered among themselves disappointedly, then trickled away. May hadn't even known specters liked pizza, but she remembered what Pumpkin's master, Arista, had said about old habits and how specters liked to hold on to them after they were dead.

"*I ain't got noboooody,*" Pumpkin nervously trilled. May nudged him hard in the arm.

"I caught these guys spying on us from the trees," Zero repeated to the spirits who were left. "And you know how we changed our motto to 'Members only.'"

One goateed spirit with a bungee cord wrapped around his neck spoke up. "Nah. You're thinking of those Members Only jackets we got from the thirdhand store in Dismal Hollow. We changed the motto to 'The more the merrier,' remember?"

"That's right," another spirit said, running her fingers through her long blond hair. She was missing part of her face. "It's 'The more the merrier,' Zero."

"Oh, yeah." Zero scratched his head, thinking.

"I interrupted Spiky Death Ball for this?" somebody muttered. The group of specters began to scatter, some running up the stairs carved into the hill that led to the top of the falls, some running over to a trampoline and leaping on it, doing levitating tricks high in the air.

The group on the boulder began to fidget, realizing they weren't in as much trouble as they'd thought. Fabbio twirled his mustache impatiently.

Finally, Zero turned a winning, good-natured smile upon

them, his gaze resting longest on Bea. "Sorry about that, dudes. I got mixed up. We're happy to have you."

"Well, we don't want to impose," Bea said, blushing.

Zero waved a hand dismissively and shook his head. "No way. That's our motto here around Risk Falls: 'Come one, come all.'"

"But I thought—," Pumpkin started, but May gave him a look that silenced him.

Zero tucked his hands deep into the pockets of his tropical shorts. "Actually, we don't have any rules here. But we *do* have parties. We're having one tonight. You should come." He winked at Beatrice, then looked around. "You want the grand tour?"

They followed Zero onto the grass and toward the lagoon.

"What is this place?" May asked. "Why is everyone all . . . ?"

"Mangled?" Zero laughed, his laughter bubbling out. "Risk Falls is the premier destination for thrill seekers in the Ever After. We all died in some kind of accident. That's how I got my name, in fact. I used to be called Arthur. Zero was my score at the surfing competition where I died. Total wipeout, man!" Zero gave the vale a sweeping, relaxed glance. "We have a bunch of people who died going over waterfalls in barrels. They're, like, the backbone of the community. But it was the surfers"—Zero winked and cleared his throat—"who founded the place. We also got skydivers, bungee jumpers, cliff divers, mountain climbers. Pretty mainstream stuff." He shrugged, his broad shoulders rolling back. "Then you got the obscure stuff. Sword swallowers, fire-eaters, crocodile hunters . . ." He paused to watch a teenager paddle by with her barrel, and they nodded at each other. Zero turned back to them. "Man, everybody's got a story." They followed him up a steep footpath along the side of the waterfall until they were about halfway to the top. Zero stepped onto a ledge and drifted to the left, disappearing into a gap between the cliff and the waterfall. "This part's tricky for first timers."

May looked at Bea, who was staring at the back of Zero's head. When she noticed May looking, she quickly looked away and then followed behind the curtain of water.

"Wow." Pumpkin sighed.

Honeycombed throughout the rock face behind the cascading water were countless nooks, deeply scooped out of the slate gray surface as if they had been balls of ice cream. Many of the hollows shone with warm blue light; some were plastered with holo-posters of surfers coasting down three-dimensional waves or mountains or climbers scaling rock faces. There were tiki torches, enormous colorful flowers, and starlight sconces. Each entrance was hung with bamboo curtains, and many of them were tied open.

"These'll be your rooms if you decide to hang," Zero said, motioning to the left.

In each room a hammock hung on either side of the hollow, with a small bamboo table on the floor in between and a skull lamp decorated with paper parasols. A tiny skull wearing a flowered headdress on the bureau opened and closed its mouth, crooning a lilting Hawaiian tune: *"Sweet Lelani, heavenly flower . . ."*

They kept moving, following Zero to the top of the falls, which afforded a beautiful view of the stars crossing the sky, the Hideous Highlands, and the mountains in the Far North.

A telescope perched on the highest crag of rock was turned toward the view below.

"We like to see if there's any trouble we can get into," Zero explained, nodding toward the telescope. "If, say, there's a band of ghouls we can sling ectoplasm balloons at or a pickup game of skull hockey. Here, take a look."

Down to the south, May could just pick out the faintest hint of an absence of glow, a shadow hanging in the air. "That's where they've been destroying towns," Zero commented, noticing the direction of her gaze. "First thing to go are the lights. Now they're putting up Cleevilvilles, which don't glow at all. It's gotten bad over the last few months."

May and Bea looked at each other. It was just as they'd feared back at Everville.

Zero hummed a little song to himself. He looked perfectly at ease.

"Are you worried?" May asked.

Zero shrugged. "Why?"

"Well, what if they come for Risk Falls?" she ventured.

"Dude, what's there to worry about? We're already dead."

"But the Bogey . . . he can turn you into nothing by sucking your spirit through his fingertips! And Bo Cleevil . . ." May didn't quite know what Bo Cleevil could do.

Zero concentrated for a moment. "I've heard of them."

May stared at him in shock. He gave her a reassuring smile.

"Look, nobody's interested in Risk Falls. We're way at the edge of the world. And if they *were* interested, they wouldn't go through all the trouble of finding us. And if they did find us, well . . ." He thought for a moment. "We're not scared. We're the risk takers, remember? We're the bravest, boldest spirits in the realm."

He studied Beatrice as he said this, as if to see her reaction. Her fine eyebrows had settled low with worry.

May wanted to ask Zero about all the spirits who were being taken away. Where were they going? Wasn't he scared for *them*? But Zero seemed so brave, so confident. Maybe he knew better.

She decided to keep her thoughts to herself.

That night, making sure no one was following her, May snuck back across the moat and spent a few hours stroking Somber Kitty so he wouldn't feel alone. She thought about the towns to the south, about all the spirits disappearing from them, and about *The Book of the Dead*.

"Meow," Kitty said, worried. Which meant: *Don't you get the feeling that something evil's on its way?*

But May, not understanding, only sighed wistfully and rubbed under his chin.

When May returned to Risk Falls, Pumpkin was asleep in her bed, his long left arm lolling off one side. May smiled, covering him up with a blanket, though she supposed it didn't matter, since ghosts didn't feel cold.

The light was still on in Bea's nook. She was in bed, reading her book on typhoid victims by the glow of a star light.

"Don't you want to take a break?" May asked.

"I've just got to finish this one thing."

The coolness of the water falling sent a nice breeze wafting in and out of the room. May fell back on a stool, kicked off her shoes, and let the breeze soothe her aching, dirty feet. Then she crawled up to the bamboo curtain and looked down into the vale. She watched the inhabitants of Risk Falls singing and playing music, gathered around a bonfire in the green bowl of the grass.

Laughter drifted up, just barely audible above the sound of the crashing water, and finally it all dwindled until only the sound of a lone ukulele remained.

"Gosh, it's a nice place, isn't it?" May asked.

"What's that?" Bea said, looking up from her book.

"Nothing. It's just, it kind of feels like the rest of the world doesn't exist here. As if even the Lady can't see us here."

Beatrice nodded distractedly, then turned the page of her book. May rested her chin on her hands, staring at the jolly spirits below. She was tempted to go down there with the others, to laugh and talk and listen to the drums.

But the outsider in May, the one from Briery Swamp who had never fit quite right, kept her tucked safely in her nook.

Chapter Six

An Invitation

Somber Kitty was curled underneath his bush, sound asleep, when he woke suddenly. He didn't know why, only he sensed something in the darkness. He sniffed the air, but whatever it was, it was far away. The tiniest vibrations in the rocky soil set his whiskers bristling.

"Meow," he said softly.

In the dusky darkness he could not see what was on its way. But he knew it was coming.

When May rose the next morning, more rested than she had been in weeks, the rest of the vale was already awake.

Spirits were sailing into the lagoon from all directions. Some were swishing down the waterslides. A man in a wet suit scarred with the mark of a shark's teeth shot out of a cannon and went careening over the sparse treetops. One spirit floated on an inner tube in the water, bedecked in sunglasses and holding a giant beach ball. It took a second glance for May to realize it was Pumpkin.

He drifted up to the shoreline on his inner tube. "Hey, May, can we move here?"

May smiled at him, then scanned the area for Fabbio and Bea. Fabbio was star bathing on the grass in full uniform, his arms crossed behind his head. Bea was talking to some spirits near the water's edge. "Well, if you hear anything, or if you see a woman who looks like she *might* have typhoid, please let me know. Even if she looks just a little peaked. Here's my tomb number." Beatrice whipped out a quill pen and a pad of parchment and scribbled down an address in Ether.

May kept walking up along the lip of the vale to a wide green field. Here, Zero and some others were playing hockey with a ball that looked like something out of a medieval torture chamber, all covered with spikes and shooting fire.

Zero ran after it like a gazelle, knocking it to one of his teammates just as he caught May's eye. He floated over.

"You wanna play? Spiky Death Ball's easy, especially if you get a good coach," he said with a wink.

May shook her head. "Zero, the reason we came here is that we need to get to the Far North right away. We were taking the train, but—"

"Yeah, we saw from the lookout post. Tracks ripped up. Bummer." Zero stuck his hands in his pockets and bobbed his head a few times.

"The poltergeists said you might help us."

"Ah. Moody little dudes. But they keep things interesting. They're always throwing stuff over the moat at us—candlesticks, pots, you know—and trying to drag us off to the Dead Sea. Sometimes we'll invite them for football. But they're horrible cheaters."

A group of spirits floated by chasing the spiky ball. They disappeared around the side of the hill. Zero hardly noticed.

"Sometimes the only thing to do when they're acting up is put 'em in a headlock. And then you give them a good noogie. They *hate* that."

May wrinkled her nose. "A noogie?"

"Yeah, you know. You slip your arm around their neck, like this."

"I know what a noogie is!" she said. But Zero slipped his frigid, ghostly arm around her neck, sending cold chills along her skin.

"Dude, there's an art to it. You really gotta lock your arms, like so, so they can't get out. Then take your fist, like this"— Zero balled up one fist—"and press hard, like this." He rubbed his fist into the top of her head. "And you gotta yell. Yelling is the most important part. Noogie! Noogie! Noogie!"

"Ouch!" May squealed, slipping loose and giggling.

Zero grinned. "Noogies. They're totally underrated. The poltergeists hate them."

May smiled, but heavier things weighed on her mind. "Anyway, about going north . . ."

Zero scratched his chin. "Well, we can't really take you there. None of us likes to leave Risk Falls. . . . It's kind of a drag out there."

"Oh." May tried not to look crestfallen. She gazed down at her feet.

"Hey. Don't stress," Zero said brightly. "If it's that big a deal, we can just send you by balloon."

"Balloon?"

Zero squinted. "Sure. I don't see why not. We have one to raid the poltergeists with sometimes. We got it from some French dude. Used to be a major balloonist when he was alive. He left us to do aerial stunts for the Shakespeare Song and Dance Revue." May immediately thought of Pumpkin. His dearest dream was to be a singer in the Shakespeare Song and Dance Revue.

"And you know our motto here at Risk Falls," Zero went on. "'Share and share alike.'"

May stifled a grin.

"C'mon," Zero said. "I'll show 'er to you."

May followed him around the side of the falls into a pretty glade overhung by rock. The balloon lay sprawled there, deflated, its big straw basket sitting upright on the grass. The balloon itself was not what she'd expected. It was shaped like a giraffe.

Zero noticed her surprise. "French dude moonlighted as a clown for a while," he explained with a shrug. "It still floats. Thing is, most spirits are tired of it. It's pretty boring, just *float-ing* around up there. And it's a lot of work. We're not so into work." He stuck his hands in his pockets and levitated, looking at the balloon.

"I'll make you a deal. Take a load off, relax for a couple days, and the balloon's all yours. We love company."

May shook her head furiously. "Uh, no, we've really got to get going."

As she said it, May looked back toward the vale and felt a pang of regret. It was so lovely here. Zero put his hand on her shoulder and gave her a look so careless and carefree, it put her worried frown to shame.

"Just kick back a bit," he urged. "Death is good."

That evening May found Pumpkin sitting by the lagoon, singing to himself.

When he saw her, he cleared his throat. "Just watching Marco Polo." He nodded toward the lagoon.

Several spirits were swimming around the lagoon calling, "Marco!"

Every once in a while a specter with a mustache and a three-pointed hat popped out of the water and yelled, "Polo! Thatsa me!"

May sat beside Pumpkin and dipped her feet in the water. Under the blue surface, the bottom of her shroud drifted off away from her feet, so that they appeared very alive. She wiggled her toes with pleasure.

She looked about her and sighed wistfully. It felt so safe here in Risk Falls.

Pumpkin noticed her thoughtfulness and moved closer beside her, dipping his own ghostly feet into the water next to hers.

"You look serious."

May smiled at him. "Do you think we need a rest, Pumpkin?"

She expected a resounding *yes!* But instead, Pumpkin looked pensive.

"You need to get home," he finally said.

May wiggled her toes some more, staring at them.

"You're right. I feel like we should leave as soon as possible."

This made Pumpkin waver. "But things are good here. Even Beatrice looks well, not so sad. . . ." Pumpkin motioned to where Bea sat on the opposite side of the pond, mending clothes for some of the Risk Fallers. She wasn't quite smiling, but as she worked, she wasn't quite wearing her thoughtful frown, either.

"We could stay for just a day or two," May offered.

Fabbio, who'd apparently been eavesdropping from where he lay on the grass, thrust one finger up into the air and, without moving his head or even opening his eyes, said, "We stay."

May looked at Pumpkin. "What do you think?"

Pumpkin nibbled a finger. "Well, we have such a big thing to do," he said. "North Farm and all of that. And it's so dangerous." He paused for a moment. "You know, I miss Arista. I miss my grave. And the beehive house."

May thought back to Arista and his cozy little house in Belle Morte, where Pumpkin had been a servant before setting out to accompany May on her journey. It had seemed so strange and unfamiliar when Pumpkin had brought her there. But if she had known then what lay ahead of her, she might have nestled into Arista's snug guest room forever. It was a far cry from the dangerous heights of the Eternal Edifice or the wilds of the Far North.

"I know the sooner we get going, the sooner I'll be home again, but . . ." He looked at May, his big black eyes thoughtful. "I'm tired of being afraid."

May reached over and gave Pumpkin's hand a squeeze. He had already faced so many fears for her. Then something else occurred to her: Kitty. They couldn't leave him hidden and alone for days. . . .

"Dudes!"

Everyone in the vale turned to see a blond pigtailed girl in scuba gear standing on the edge of the lagoon, her arms wrapped around a squirming Somber Kitty. "I found a *living cat*." She nodded toward the bundle in her arms, then beamed at everyone.

May's heart stood still.

"Can we keep it?"

The Risk Fallers swept toward Kitty. May leaped up to come to his aid.

"Awesome!" somebody yelled. Somber Kitty let out a low meow and gave May a pitiful glance.

May breathed a sigh of relief. Nobody seemed to mind that he was a fugitive. She turned to look at Pumpkin, Fabbio, and Bea, who'd come over to investigate. "Okay. We can stay a *few* days. Three. If you want." She looked at Beatrice for approval. Pumpkin deserved a break. They all did.

Bea looked unsure. She gazed at the faces of the other two, looking like she wanted to protest. But then she softened. "Well, if the others want to, I suppose we could. . . ."

Pumpkin and Fabbio let out hoots. Across the grass Somber Kitty let out another meow, but nobody heard. Instinctively, May thought back to her telep-a-gram: *Never forget that the way back is forward.* But she chose to ignore that for now, just for the moment.

"Three days," she repeated. "Tops."

What could happen in three days?

Chapter Seven

The Forgetting Lagoon

For several minutes a cloud of dust had been growing just south of Cleevilville #135, announcing the approach of a group of riders. The cloud grew and grew, until the riders came to a halt just outside the town gates.

When the cloud settled, six figures, clad in tattered red riding jackets and puffs of yellowed lace at their throats, emerged from the dust. Each sat astride a heaving, snarling gargoyle and held a riding crop in one hand and a pair of braided reins in the other.

The riders circled the abandoned railroad tracks, studying the ground leading in and out of the town. It wasn't long before one gestured to a single pair of footprints in the dirt. Only Live Ones leave footprints.

Without delay, the Wild Hunters whipped their mounts into motion, following the tracks north.

The group settled into the paradisiacal vale as snugly as peas in rice. Captain Fabbio introduced an Italian game called Who's Got the Spumoni? which he won most of the time because he kept changing the rules. Beatrice, unable to get her hands on any new books or even one newspaper—as these things seemed to be absent from Risk Falls entirely—mended every piece of clothing in the vale, then started in on other projects: polishing the surfboards, dusting the tiki torches, scrubbing the ledge that led behind the water. Pumpkin and Somber Kitty starting going on walks together, which surprised everyone. Somber Kitty would pass by May's doorway, turning occasionally to flick his tail at Pumpkin, hurrying him up. Pumpkin would drift along behind and give a quick wave to May as he floated past.

May watched these comings and goings with a secret smile. From what she could gather, Pumpkin had finally recognized Somber Kitty's willingness to listen to everything he had to say, and Somber Kitty had begun to appreciate Pumpkin's optimism. From time to time, Somber Kitty would prance back up to the room in a huff and leap onto May's lap, after some unknown quarrel. And Pumpkin would scowl at him all through that evening's activities—the slippery rock relay, the ball of acid toss, the tightrope race across the ravine— and accuse May of taking his side. But inevitably, they would traipse off together the next morning as if nothing had happened at all.

Fabbio set up a cleaning detail to clear the vale of ghost weeds. Everyone who agreed to help, which meant Beatrice and May, met him at five every morning.

Each day most of the Risk Falls inhabitants, no matter how many limbs they were missing, took to the lake and floated on their backs. Only Somber Kitty sat on the edge, growling at the ripples, letting out a woeful chorus of "Mew. Meow. Meay."

Having lost his owner to a water demon, he had more reason than most cats to be suspicious of water.

May marveled at the bravery of the spirits of Risk Falls. They weren't scared of anything: not falling off cliffs or catching on fire or getting shot through with arrows (they shot one another quite frequently). They seemed to enjoy being dead with reckless abandon. Taken with the idea, May designed a barrel with rudders for the spirits to steer over the falls. She also forged a shortcut to the top of the cliffs that the others had never noticed, invented a quick and easy way to reattach missing parts with paper clips, and showed everyone how to teach a cat to dance. (Even though it would never come in handy, her students were delighted.) But the thing the specters of Risk Falls liked most of all about May Bird was that she told the best stories.

She had told them only to Pumpkin at first—stories about her mom, about Somber Kitty the warrior cat, about Briery Swamp and the people she imagined had once lived there. She spun stories about White Moss Manor and its previous owners, including a woman named Bertha Brettwaller, rumored to have had horrible breath and to have walked out of the house one morning looking for wild garlic, never to return. Adding details like this here and there, he listened raptly to May's histories, Somber Kitty snoozing at her side.

Presently, they were joined by a couple of spirits who happened to overhear, and the number kept growing until the entire population of Risk Falls was gathered in the vale every night to hear May recall the Eternal Edifice, the New Egyptians, the Bogey, and a psychic beekeeper named Arista. They were good stories already, but May added flourishes and embellishments, colorful descriptions, and passionate hand gestures, until every listener was under her spell, every ear trained on her every syllable. May found that when she was telling these stories, she forgot to be shy at all.

Beatrice, meanwhile, woke each morning to find bouquets littered outside her door from various admirers. Also, piles of laundry. Both made her flush with pleasure.

Oddly, on the fourth day not one of the travelers remembered that today was the day they'd planned to leave. Somber Kitty alone paced impatiently at the edge of the trees, trying to catch May's eye. Whenever he did, he tried to wave her into the woods with his tail. But May, dripping in the invisible shroud that covered her sparkly bathing suit, which was slowly starting to lose its sparkle, would only smile at him in a lazy, relaxed way and go for another jump into the lagoon.

May learned to shoot an arrow. To swing on a rope. To do a back handspring.

If anyone had noticed that she didn't float like everyone else or that she was more colorful than the average ghost, they didn't say anything. And May began to think of herself not as a Live One, but as just another spirit of Risk Falls.

Bea found herself needed and adored. Fabbio had found good-natured spirits, including Marco Polo himself, always willing to play by his rules. And Pumpkin had found a place to frolic.

"May," Bea said one morning when they were floating in the lagoon, "it's odd, but sometimes I don't even remember why we're here."

May crossed her arms beneath her head on her inner tube. "I know. Do you think that's bad?"

Bea shrugged, then yawned. The two floated along in silence for some time.

The day drifted away.

Their reason for being there, and their memories of the world beyond Risk Falls, became hazier and hazier. And North Farm, with its ambiguous promise of home, grew farther and farther away.

Outside Necromancy Nancy's Snack Shoppe, a figure in a red coat climbed down from his mount. With oily slickness, he held up one arm to indicate that the others should take care. With a tiny tilt of his head, he nodded to the front door.

As the six crept toward the shack, a screech issued from inside, followed by a hurtling teakettle. It flew through the window and whistled in the direction of the first hunter, who caught it with one white-gloved hand. He lunged toward the doorway and disappeared inside, dragging his attacker out into the open, pinning it to the ground under one black boot.

The poltergeist squirmed and howled but could not pry itself loose.

A deep whisper issued from the hunter's black lips. "Mecka-lecka hiney ho?"

That was poltergeist for "Where are they?"

Chapter Eight

The Wild Hunt

May stared at the invitation lying on the hammock with breathless anticipation: *Come to a dress-up shindig. Tonight!*

May and Somber Kitty had had a few small affairs in May's room back home. And May had shared in cupcake parties at school (though usually the cupcakes ran out, and May only got to scrape the icing off the box). But she had never been to a shindig.

That afternoon she had created a warrior costume out of silver beads, a black sheet she had borrowed from Zero, the flowers from the plant in her room, and, of course, her death shroud. Now she was letting Bea paint her face in blue and green streaks with ink squeezed from the ghost weeds. Bea had already pulled her hair back in a tight braided ponytail and stuck some feathers into the hair band.

"Just one more," Bea said, grinning. "There." She turned May toward the mirror so she could see herself.

The braid made her look like she had hardly any hair. The lines of the war paint were crooked and made her look bluish and quite dead, and the feathers tilted at weird, floppy angles.

"Do you like it?" Bea asked, clasping her hands together unsurely.

"Oh, yes." May's heart sank, though. Bea had made her look like a boy.

Bea beamed. Her own blond hair was fashioned into a tender flounce that complemented the blue of her eyes and the pink of her gentle cheeks. May had been hoping for something more like that.

"How do I look?" Bea asked.

May grinned. Bea always looked beautiful. "I think *Zero* will think you look *very* pretty."

Beatrice turned pink, sniffed, then gave her hair a messy toss. "I certainly don't care." But as they walked out of the room, May noticed she patted her curls again to make them neat.

Down in the vale, echoes of cracking coconuts rang against the cliffs. Bongos and guitars came levitating down into the canyon in the arms of their levitating owners, and a bonfire was lit by the lake, where everyone was gathered. Zero, wearing his usual grin and a T-shirt that read DEATH IS GOOD, said that it was a tradition on festival nights for everyone to get up and recount how they'd died.

The stories of daring deaths stretched and stitched themselves through the night. One woman had fallen down a crevice in the Andes and had never emerged. Another had been taming lions in Africa and turned her back on them for a moment, dazzled by an unfortunately timed Serengeti sunset. One salty old veteran had been traversing Papua New Guinea on foot when he'd waded into a nest of hungry leeches. While these stories were told, the bongo drummers drummed.

Some spirits had tales of adventures in the Afterlife as well. Several had met up with poltergeists. One had slept in a seemingly deserted grotto, only to wake to find he had been hog-tied by goblins and was being dragged to the Dead Sea as a souvenir. Fortunately, it was Fashion Week in Glow-So, the avant-garde garment district of Ether, and the goblins had come across a sale. They'd forgotten about him long enough for him to chew off his ropes.

At the end of the story Pumpkin shot up. "May is supposed to save the Ever After from certain doom."

Everyone went silent for a moment. Pumpkin looked about uncertainly, the color rising on his pale, wrinkled cheeks. Somebody said, "Cool." A couple of spirits stood up and drifted away. Another began to strum on a guitar.

"That reminds me, my cousin got into a fistfight with a zombie at the Pit of Despair."

And so the spirits continued with their stories. Pumpkin looked rather deflated until a round of singing started up. Apparently, the song was very popular in the Afterlife, because even Fabbio knew the words. They both joined in.

> "In our island paradise
> That volcano sure looked nice
> You fell in and so did I
> I screamed once, but you screamed twice
> The lava was hotta than any spice
> In our island paradise."

Pumpkin's singing rang out louder than the others, but nobody minded because of his beautiful singing voice. Bea sang along, gazing at the others. May watched silently.

"Why don't you sing?" Bea eventually asked her, happy in the moment.

"Oh, I can't sing," May said, shaking her head. That wasn't exactly true. She sang along with *The Sound of Music* sometimes, but only when she was alone. And she sang very badly. Though, now that she thought about it, she probably hadn't been alone at all. She had only recently discovered Pumpkin had been haunting her house for years.

"Oh, go on, anybody can sing," Beatrice encouraged her gently.

May smiled, but even when the chorus came around a second and third time, she kept her smiling mouth closed.

A few spirits got up to dance. Zero spun by a few times, dancing in a jokey, kicky, dashing kind of way. On the third pass he yanked Beatrice up in one deft motion, spinning her under his arm, the two floating lopsidedly off into the crowd. Beatrice, shooting a *Please help me* face at May, nevertheless glided gracefully as a feather. A smile snuck across her face from one ear to the other, which she turned to the ground to hide.

May half wanted to be asked to dance and half didn't. She tapped her feet. When the boy with the alligator scars looked at her across the grass and winked, May looked away quickly and frowned, shy. Somber Kitty, who loved to dance more than anything except for May, leaped up and did some interpretive ballet. Pumpkin and May laughed and clapped.

A limbo contest was held, and Somber Kitty won. But then something seemed to turn him serious. He sniffed the air solemnly and retired to May's side, looking worried.

The bonfire flickered on the water. May hugged her knees tighter, watching through her big eyes. "What is it, Kitty?"

Kitty stared at her and whispered, "Meay."

May looked back out at the dancers, then back at him. "Is something wrong?"

Suddenly, the spirits on the grass went silent and still.

"What's everybody—?" Pumpkin began loudly, but Zero held his finger to his lips.

"Shhh!" He floated onto his knees and pressed his ear against the ground. A moment later Zero sat back up, nodding at the others, his eyes wide and round. He smiled from ear to ear.

He stood, reached out, and grabbed May's hand. "Something's coming!"

In a sudden burst, every spirit within hearing distance dropped what they were doing and swarmed onto the cliffs like ants, disappearing behind the falls. Before May and the others could react, they began to reappear, holding various vehicles in their hands: rickety old scooters, unicycles, pogo sticks. Zero himself squeaked to a halt in front of the gang on a dirt bike, twisting the handles impatiently.

"Well, come on, then." Zero yanked May by the hand and pulled her onto the back of his bike. "Hold on!"

"Kitty!" May looked behind her as she was spirited away on the bike. Kitty was running after them.

May clutched the back of Zero's T-shirt as he navigated the bike.

"Stop! Wait! Why are we going *toward* it?" she yelled, pushing onto her tiptoes to get close to Zero's ear.

Zero banked the bike sharply around a rock and they wobbled, May clinging tighter to his middle. "*Thrills,*" he called back. "Most of the stuff we do gets old, since we're dead and all already. Last time we had a good shake-up was when a bunch of goblins were looking for some Live One. Bogus Breath Brenda or something."

May's stomach gave a little lurch.

"But what if they—?"

"Don't worry. It'll be great." He looked over his shoulder at May and caught a glimpse of her face. "Probably just some ghouls. They're easy to mess with. You'll see."

May balked. *Just some ghouls?* "But, Zero—"

"Hey, don't worry! Death is good!"

May clenched her hands tighter as they rode into the darkness.

The cyclists came to a halt at the very edge of a rolling, rocky pasture, punctuated on one side, far in the distance, with a tiny stone church silhouetted in the starlight, surrounded by a sprawling, abandoned cemetery. The spirits hovered on their bikes steadily—about twenty in number—making a long row. Several bikes had two or more riders, their legs hanging all askew as they perched on handlebars and crowded onto seats. All eyes watched the horizon. May watched too, over Zero's shoulder.

And then, from somewhere in the dark ahead, came the sound of an invisible bugle. A rustle went through the crowd.

A moment later, muted and barely audible, came the *thud, thud, thud* of feet. It sounded like they belonged to some huge animal.

Tiny shadows moved on the horizon, so small that at first May couldn't tell for sure if they were actually there. The line of cyclists bristled again, rubbing their hands together, testing their pedals, leaning into their pogo sticks, turning their handlebars just slightly.

May looked at Beatrice, sitting primly sidesaddle on another bike, curled against her rider and squinting into the distance with a frown. May looked behind her for Somber Kitty, but he was far behind them—still running, but unable to keep up.

"Steady," Zero whispered. "Steady . . ."

As the shadows up ahead came into focus, a surprised murmur went through the crowd.

On the horizon were six dark shapes. They rode astride six winged gargoyles with flames spouting from their nostrils.

Zero gasped. "Oh!"

Sighting the line of bikers, one of the figures let out a blood-curdling screech. Then they launched into a full-on gallop.

May's arms and legs went numb. She watched in horror as the figures hurtled toward them, becoming more and more distinct. Six horrible faces emerged from the darkness. They were a ghastly blue, gaunt and lifeless, with sunken cheeks, twisted, toothless mouths, and gaping holes for eyes. Long, oily black hair hung out of their black top hats. They spurred on the gargoyles beneath them with their riding crops.

"Pull back!" Zero turned his bike on a dime and began to pedal furiously. All around them, the line of Risk Fallers erupted back in the direction they'd come, skidding and swerving, hopping, falling into their pedals and pushing ahead with all their might.

Behind them, May could hear the *huff-huff* of gargoyle breath. Zero hit a rock, and the bike went wobbly. As they lurched, May couldn't help but fling a look over her shoulder.

The riders weren't far behind. They were executing flips in the air, flying sideways and even upside down.

"Faster, Zero!" May screamed. Most of the other cyclists had disappeared into the trees. May searched the remaining crowd for Beatrice, or Pumpkin or Fabbio, but they had disappeared too.

Zero veered left, then right, sending May wobbling and scrabbling her fingers in the folds of his T-shirt to hang on. She felt herself start to slide backward off the seat. "Zeeeeeeeeeeeeeeeeee . . . !"

Zero reached an arm around to grab her, but it was too late. May felt the seat disappear beneath her, and suddenly she was tumbling backward through the air, landing on the grass with a hard thump. Her death shroud fell open on one side.

The plains went silent. Those who were biking away came to a halt and looked over their shoulders at the living girl, her shroud fallen away. Zero circled in an about-face on his bike to stare, his mouth dropping open. Slowly, May sat up. Behind her, across the plain, the Wild Hunters had stopped too.

The leader's eyeless eyes stared at her, frozen. And then he shrieked and kicked his gargoyle forward.

May leaped up, unsteady on her feet, her shroud now hanging limp from her neck. For a moment May met Zero's eyes. His, for the first time, were filled with terror.

"May, run!"

May was frozen in place watching the riders come toward her. And then she looked frantically about. There was the church at the edge of the field. *There!*

May ran toward it full tilt. Behind her, she could hear Zero and some of the others racing to catch up, perhaps to bait the hunters.

She hit the front of the church at a sprint, not daring to look behind her. She yanked hard on the door, but it wouldn't give. Turning, she pressed against it with her back. Only three of the terrifying riders were racing in her direction now. The others fanned out behind them, blocking her escape. She dashed around the side of the church and into the cemetery.

The tombstones were as crumbled and crooked as bad teeth. May chose a stone tall enough to hide her—sculpted in the shape of an angel—and crouched behind it. She curled herself into a ball and waited.

Several moments went by, and May began to think that, miraculously, the riders had gone past the church. She peered out from her hiding spot. She could just see, through one of the church windows, a smallish sliver of purplish face.

May gasped and ducked behind the stone again, bending her chin close to her knees and trying not to breathe too loud. Soon she heard the whispery rustling of the riders drifting into the cemetery. She peeked around a second time, just barely. The three hunters had dismounted and were floating among the stones, the mist rising from the graves around them. One seemed to glance in her direction. As smoothly and slickly as a snake, he drifted toward her.

May curled back behind the stone and bit her bottom lip firmly. She looked around for some kind of weapon to defend herself. There was nothing. She held her breath and sat stock-still.

A few seconds went by. Then, slowly, a white, withered hand reached around the side of the tombstone. It touched May's cheek, then, feeling, moved across her nose.

May opened her mouth and bit down.

Screeeeeeeeeeeeeeeeeeeeeeeeeeeeeeech!

May didn't think. She acted. She leaped forward and wrapped her arm around the hunter's neck. Then she rubbed her knuckles against his head as hard as she could, yelling, "Noogie! Noogie! Noogie!"

The hunter let out a shocked gargling sound, trying to escape but unable to loose himself from May's locked grasp. When he finally stumbled backward, his oily hair making him too slick to hold any longer, May moved quickly. She cocked back her left foot and kicked his rotten left shin.

Screeeeeeeeeeeeeeeeeeeeeeeeech! The hunter reeled backward, clutching his leg. Hobbled, half crouched, and completely bewildered, he turned and zipped past his two companions—who were levitating across the graveyard, utterly shocked—knocking down small tombstones in his wake, his gargoyle following on his heels.

Stunned, May turned and ran the other way.

Chapter Nine

The Carnival at the Edge of the World

THIS WAY FOR A GREAT VIEW.

May came to a sudden halt, turning to look behind her and breathing hard. She had been running for as long as she could, turning this way and that. And it looked like it had worked. There was no sign of the hunters. But now, she realized, she was perfectly lost.

May turned back to the sign that had caused her to stop. It hung from a post beside a tunnel carved into a rocky hill. It seemed suspicious, appearing as it did in the middle of nowhere.

She cast another glance behind her. Surely, Somber Kitty would sniff her trail and find her. Until then, she resolved to go on. She set her chin and made her way into the tunnel. A tiny imprint in the stone said CUSTOM WALLS BY HADRIAN. A few feet farther a larger sign read AMUSEMENTS, REFRESHMENTS, THE REST OF THE UNIVERSE, THIS WAY. A moment later the tunnel poured her out into starlight again. May went to take another step forward, but she gasped and leaped backward instead.

There was nothing in front of her. Nothing but black space

and billions of stars zooming past. She had reached a ledge of some sort, and only space lay beyond it.

May steadied herself and crept up to the edge, leaning forward gingerly and peering over. The rocky cliff face ran in a straight wall downward, without end for as far as the eye could see.

"The edge of the world," May whispered, her breath quite taken away. She stared out at the vast space for several minutes, unable to move. Eventually, a bit of light drew her attention left. There she noticed a walkway winding along the ledge and a crumbled stone wall, disintegrated in places, hugging its right side. The walkway curved around a hill and disappeared in a halo of light to the south. Letting out a deep breath, May followed it.

Shortly, it brought her to another dazzling sight. On a wide shelf overlooking the cliff stood a cluster of tattered pink-and-red-striped circus tents, all looking like they were about to collapse. Each tent was festooned with green and purple lightbulbs, twinkling and blinking and sparkling as coolly as the moon.

The tents appeared to be deserted, but just in case, May adjusted her death shroud as she came to a glowing banner that arched over the walkway.

CARN V L AT THE EDG F T E W RLD

The carnival was not nearly as grand as it had looked on the billboards she had seen. Instead of enormous attractions, there were these tents. No Ferris wheel soared above—only a small mechanical wheel in a clearing up ahead that spun just feet above the ground, with two seats. The Tunnel of Terror looked to be a *Molehill* of Terror.

The tents looked ancient, and many of the lights were either burned out or crushed. May shuffled up to one and peered in through a rent in the filmy fabric. She gasped. Inside was a ride with skeletal elephants wearing little yellow hats. She shuffled to the next tent, which held something called a Living Castle, with tiny metalwork people peeking out of its windows, their little metal arms waving, their little metal legs attached to wire pulleys that moved them forward and back into the shadows of the house, over and over. A third held It's a Small Realm After All, a diorama of the whole of the Ever After that gave a bird's-eye view of the Dead Sea, the City of Ether, the Hideous Highlands, and more. Upon closer inspection, May realized the diorama was full of motion. She leaned forward breathlessly to examine the tiny boats moving up and down the Styx Streamway, the hundreds of translucent pin-dot spirits moving around the City of Ether, a minuscule roller coaster zipping along its tracks in the Pit of Despair Amusement Park, and a darkly rippling Dead Sea.

Nibbling a pinky nail, May searched the southern end of the diorama for the small town of Belle Morte, but only the Catacomb Cliffs had been reproduced, and May touched them gently, thinking of Lucius.

She wove along the circus attractions, soon finding herself a few yards away from a squat building fronted by a sprawling, yawning porch overhung by a blinking neon sign on stilts that read EAT AT THE ETERNAL RESTAURANT! The porch butted right up against the cliff's edge and was dotted with several view-finders—tall, rusted metal posts with binoculars at the top, like May had seen in postcards of the Grand Canyon. She climbed the rickety porch stairs and inspected one more closely. A tiny engraving read SPY ON STARS BILLIONS OF LIGHT-YEARS AWAY! FEEL LIKE YOU'RE THERE!

May smoothed back her bangs and gazed into the view-finder. It was like swimming in the ocean, then looking under-water with a pair of goggles. Suddenly, the stars surrounding the Ever After came into focus.

BETA 7894553 IS FOR LOVERS!
IF YOU LIVED ON BETELGEUSE, YOU'D BE HOME BY NOW!

May pulled back and squinted at the sky. Nothing but tiny pinpoint stars. She looked back through the viewfinder and tilted it upward. Closer, just above her head, a long glowing banner of light being cast skyward from the Ever After read BORED OF THE ENTIRE UNIVERSE? TRY THE AFTERLIFE!

Wow. May had had no idea the universe was full of so many ads. She swept the sky, hoping to get a glimpse of Earth, but she guessed it was too far away to see. May was too deeply lost in thought to notice the figure hovering nearby until it floated close enough to touch her.

Rumor had it that Commander Berzerko had been let out of her pen. That very morning the Wild Hunters had burst into South Place crying for their mommies and had galloped straight for the Bogey's bedroom. Apparently, in their long and sordid careers tracking and trapping prey, they had never once come across a prize that fought back. Especially with noogies.

Now the Bogey, it was whispered, had been forced to resort to the unthinkable. And all the Dark Spirits of South Place closed their casket doors a little tighter, looked over their slimy shoulders a little more often, and slept a little less soundly (though they still continued to snore). They were sure, every time they turned a corner on the Screamerplatz or walked along the banks of the Corkscrew River or wound their way toward their graves at midnight to haunt Earth, that Commander Berzerko would be there, ready to do . . . well, the thing that Commander Berzerko did best.

And though they had good reason to be fearful, they need not have gone through all the trouble, for by the first evening of her release, Commander Berzerko was not in South Place at all, but at a teleporter in the abandoned town of Cleevilville #135.

The commander stepped out of the booth and took a good look around.

Her fluffy black fur stood high around her pudgy figure, lush and voluminous. Her long black tail bobbed coquettishly, like a pom-pom. Her fur was more than four inches long and standing up in all directions, making her look like a round black marshmallow or a fluffy black Butterball turkey on Thanksgiving Day.

A tiny, delicate pink bow was positioned jauntily by one black ear. Her whiskers were long and wistful, her eyes wide, green, and irresistible. She wore a glittering collar of black diamonds.

She lifted her head to sniff the air, revealing the glossy white teeth poking out of her jowls, and said one simple word: "Meow."

With the scent of the living cat fresh in her nose, Commander Berzerko headed north.

Chapter Ten

The Stranger

A re you looking for something?"

May jolted and stepped backward, tightening her death shroud. "Oh!"

The spirit wore a dark, wide-brimmed hat, its shadow hiding his eyes and cheeks and revealing only a rough, scarred chin and a pair of curled, dry lips. The lips rose in a sneer.

"Didn't mean to startle you," he said. May rocked back slightly on her heels. His breath smelled sour.

"That's okay." She gulped, blinking at him, her throat dry. He nodded toward the viewfinder.

"I see you were taking in the view."

May swallowed. "Uh-huh. Yes. It's, um . . . pretty?"

He let out a low, gravelly laugh. He drifted past her and cast a desultory glance beyond the cliff.

"I don't find it all that pretty myself. Rather annoyingly"—he raised his arms and lowered them in a graceful shrug—"vast, I think. Too much space for me. Or maybe it's too little of *me* for all that space. It makes me feel . . . small. Like a speck." He turned toward her, and his lip curled again. "Do you ever feel like a speck, boy?"

May swallowed. It took her a moment to realize that she was still in her warrior costume and that, indeed, she still looked like a boy. And then she tried to focus on the question. She remembered how far away the mountains of the north had seemed to her just a few days ago—how the distance made her feel like a speck. "Sometimes," she answered.

The stranger's mouth turned down gently and coldly. He looked out at the stars again. Something about him made May very sad.

"We *are* just stardust after all." He looked at May, then let out a cold, bitter laugh.

"What do you mean?" May ventured.

He looked at her as if she should already know the answer. "That is what all creatures great and small are made of. Leftover stardust. An atom exploded, and all the dust became the planets, the stars . . . and us. That's all anything amounts to."

May considered this. She actually liked the idea that she might be made out of stars. She passed her hand over her death shroud thoughtfully.

"You never answered my question."

"Question?"

"Are you *looking* for something?"

"Oh, no, nooo, just . . ." She looked at her feet. She shifted from one to the other. "Sightseeing."

"Oh?" He focused on her intently now. His angular features—the ones she could see—struck her for the first time as very handsome for someone *old*. Older than old. "How unique. Most spirits stopped coming here a long time ago. You must be a singular sort of spirit."

"I guess you could call me that," May warbled.

"I see." The stranger nodded, then smiled, seeming to approve. "I see you are a loner. I like to be alone too." He laughed, and his laughter crackled with bitterness. "Two peas in a pod . . ."

May realized he was waiting for her name. She cast about, trying to think of one. It didn't occur to her to use her own. Instinct told her not to. She looked toward the circus tents. "Dumbo?"

"Dumbo?"

May nodded, wanting to throw herself over the cliff for how *dumbo* she really was.

"A singular name for a singular boy," the man said.

"Yes, sir."

"I like you." He nodded. "Yes, yes I do. And, you know, I don't really like anyone."

May didn't know what to say to that.

The stranger drifted right up to the cliff's edge and kicked a stone over the side, watching it drop. His shoulders sank slightly. "Vast," he muttered. Again, May had the curious feeling of being sorry for and scared of him all at once.

He turned back to her. "Aren't you going to ask what brings me here? Make conversation? That's what spirits do. Don't you find me interesting?"

"Um, what brings you here?" May asked obligingly.

He rubbed his chin scar with one grimy, weathered hand. "Looking for something."

"What?" May asked, her stomach churning.

"A *little* thing, really. A girl."

"Oh?" May said. A tiny, almost imperceptible movement

drew her eyes toward one of the tents. There, crouched and peering around one of the flaps, was a pair of green kitty eyes, in a hairless kitty face. May's heart did a high dive.

When she returned her gaze to the stranger, he was eyeing her thoughtfully. She could see just the faintest glow of his eyes from deep underneath the shadow of his hat.

"She's alive."

"Oh."

"She's very small."

"Really?" May squeaked.

"And she's got black hair."

"Oh?"

"She is traveling with a cat."

May couldn't find her voice to say one more thing.

The man watched her for a moment, frowning. His fingers jumped and danced at his sides, agitated.

"There's a house ghost with them. And maybe a couple of others."

May managed to nod.

"I've been told she's been destroyed. On the edge of the City of Ether."

The stranger scanned the horizon again, and May's eyes shot to Somber Kitty. Only his nose protruded from the tent flap now, sniffing.

The stranger sighed. "I *feel* that it's not true. But then"—here, his mouth became slack, unsure—"the girl is probably nothing. I tend to be somewhat . . . paranoid."

His voice, as it fell on the last word, filled May with a deep, strange sadness. May couldn't find the thoughts or the words or the voice to say anything. Her heart danced an achy-breaky jig under her ribs.

"There, Dumbo." He took hold of May's shoulders, his icy hands sending cold chills straight down her spine, and turned her toward the precipice, pointing to the dots of light in the distance. "There's Earth." May squinted, but she couldn't tell which one he was pointing at. "We are *connected*. We are Earth's shadow, like the negative of a photograph. But one day Earth will be *my* shadow. I'll be very popular. And then I'll never be alone. Which reminds me . . ." The stranger lowered his arm.

"Reminds you of what?" May asked, turning back around.

But the stranger was gone.

May looked about for several seconds, then clutched the front of her bathing suit with one hand, breathing deeply.

She walked over to Somber Kitty and lifted him into her arms, feeling dread to the bottom of her soul.

"We've got to get north," she whispered to Kitty, placing him on the ground and letting him point the way back to Risk Falls.

That night Ellen Bird stood on her wide front lawn and looked at the stars.

Days had passed since she'd found the briars in May's overalls. And every day it seemed as if the woods were inviting her in, whispering that the briars, somehow, knew where May had gone. But something kept Ellen from venturing into the trees. Something that sent shivers down her spine.

Sighing, she wished upon one of the millions of stars above. One that seemed to flicker a little more dimly than the rest, like a patron star of lost causes. She wished that she would find what she was looking for.

Tomorrow, she promised herself, she would look for it beyond the endless briars.

On a rise that drooped slowly toward the moat surrounding Risk Falls, a tiny figure stalked into view. It was fluffy and round and wore a diamond collar that glinted in the starlight.

"Puuuurrrrrrrrr," Commander Berzerko said, sniffing the air, her keen slitted eyes scanning the trees for any sign of life beyond them. But it was no matter: The scent of the girl and her cat were so strong, so close, that the commander could have found them in the dark. She pawed the ground eagerly, making muffins in the dirt, sharpening her claws. This would be easy.

She sauntered a few steps forward, then began to run.

Part Two

Into the Far North

Chapter Eleven

Two Cats

I think I'm allergic to something," Bea said tightly, pulling a hanky from her pocket and dabbing at her eyes gently.

The group of travelers stood near the big straw basket of the giraffe-shaped hot air balloon, saying their good-byes. Pumpkin snuffled loudly every few seconds as tears ran out of his droopy eyes.

"I have made a poem for good-bye," Fabbio said, standing up straight. Everyone braced themselves.

> *"Tortellini, pizza pie*
> *I have something in my eye*
> *Is a teardrop, big and blue*
> *Because we saying toodle-loo."*

On these last words, Fabbio's voice became choked and he touched his fingers to his lips, bowing his head and closing his eyes.

Zero grinned. "Listen, May Bird. Your escape from the hunters was truly spectacular." He stuck his hands in the pockets of his long shorts. "And it's so cool that you're alive. What's more risky than that in the Afterlife?"

May blushed. To her amazement, when she and Kitty had returned to Risk Falls, she had been set upon by cheering spirits. No one had expressed a moment's concern about what had been revealed back at the Wild Hunt. In fact, like Zero, everyone had been quite thrilled to have a living girl in their midst. In the fray, May had not told anyone about the Eternal Restaurant or the stranger she had met there. Oddly enough, she felt it was an event that belonged only to her, like a deep dark secret.

Somber Kitty sat beside her on the ground, guarding the basket like a lion and staring southeast into the highlands. Occasionally, he let out a tiny growl and wove between May's legs impatiently. May scratched the backs of her knees, flattered and horribly embarrassed. "Zero, you heard what I said. About Bo Cleevil. Risk Falls could be next. You'll . . . do something, won't you?"

Zero eyed her seriously for a moment, then gave her a punch on the shoulder and a careless grin. "No worries, dude. Everything's cool here."

May bit her lip and looked at Beatrice, who frowned with worry. Clearly, the inhabitants of this place, like so much of the Ever After, weren't as worried as they should be. May climbed into the basket, which was laden with sleeping bags, camping supplies, and other gifts from the spirits of Risk Falls.

"Queen Bea," Zero said, taking Beatrice's hand gently in his. Bea looked up to the sky as if she saw something very interesting above. But when Zero lifted her hand to his lips and kissed it, she stared at him, her eyes wide, a smile bursting out on her flushed face.

And then she swiped away a little tear as she followed the others into the balloon, trying to climb in as daintily as she could.

Only Somber Kitty remained on the grass. "C'mon, Kitty. What are you waiting for?" May coaxed.

Kitty glanced at her over his shoulder, then stood up and looked into the distance again, his tail sticking straight up. "Meow."

"Come, little Kitty," Fabbio said, leaning over and lifting him by the armpits. Kitty dangled from his hands like an old shoelace, still staring southeast. He let out a sound like May had never heard before, something between a moan and a growl.

May took him from Fabbio and held him close, looking at him, concerned. "What is it?" She followed his gaze toward the horizon, beyond the moat.

There *was* something there. She couldn't tell whether it was far away or just really small.

"Well," Zero said, "catch you later." He untied one of the ropes holding down the balloon. With a *thwap!* and a *zwing!* the basket tilted far to the left.

"This no problem," Fabbio said, taking hold of the burner that steered the balloon and thrusting it forward. The basket jarred even farther left, until it was almost sideways. Kitty went flying out of May's arms, landing on all fours on the grass and shaking himself off.

"Kitty!"

May managed to scoop the cat into her arms just as the balloon started floating backward.

Thwap! Zero untied the other rope. The balloon teetered there for a moment, as if it needed to rev itself up in order to ascend. Its occupants looked around dazedly. By this time, whatever was approaching them had crossed the moat and was dashing across the vale.

"What *is* that?" Beatrice said, pointing. May could see now— it *was* small and actually not far away at all. It looked like . . .

"Well, I'll *be* . . . ," one Risk Falls spirit exclaimed.

The creature was zipping toward them, its tail flouncing out behind it.

May could feel Somber Kitty's heart beating against his ribs. His fur stood up all around. He let out the loudest, meanest growl May had ever heard escape his lips.

"Is that . . . a pink bow?" Pumpkin asked. They were still only inches above the ground, drifting slowly backward as Fabbio tried to steer.

The creature approached the balloon far faster than anyone could have imagined. One moment it was a hundred yards away, and the next, it was only a matter of feet.

Somber Kitty hissed and spat wildly, his whole body shaking.

"Now for turning up the burner," Fabbio muttered to himself, casting an indifferent glance at the tiny creature racing toward them. The rest of the group watched in awe.

Then, inexplicably, when it was still several feet away, the creature leaped. It leaped higher and farther than any leap May had ever seen, seeming to *fly* at the balloon, one paw poised in the air, the claws extended and directed at the leg of the giraffe.

"Ah!" Fabbio pushed something, and the balloon accelerated

straight up. The creature's paw fell just short of the balloon, and it went plummeting toward the ground beneath them. A great howl of frustration issued from its throat as it landed on all fours, staring upward, its green eyes glinting.

The rest of the travelers peered over the edge of the basket, befuddled, as they rose into the air.

Fabbio, finally, looked over the edge with interest. "What a cute little kitty."

Everyone but Somber Kitty agreed.

Chapter Twelve

The Petrified Pass

May and Kitty went tumbling across the grass, rolling lopsidedly along until they ran up against a giant rock and came to a dead stop. May sat up, rubbing her head, trying to get her bearings. Somber Kitty let out a groan and tumbled out of his papoose. The hot air balloon lay deflated along the rocky ground, the basket turned sideways.

Pumpkin lay in a blubbering heap a few feet away. Beatrice was helping Captain Fabbio stand up and brushing off her dress.

"This not my best landing," Fabbio said, flapping his hands against his medals to dust them off. In fact, after hours of soaring above the empty highlands, the balloon had suddenly and without warning descended downward, dumping them out in an unseemly mess.

Recovering themselves, everyone looked in May's direction. Pumpkin let out a scream. Bea's hands flew over her mouth. May turned to see what they were looking at, then gulped.

It wasn't a rock she had plowed into—or at least not a rock in the traditional sense. It was, in fact, a giant skull, standing at least six feet high, its huge tooth-addled mouth gaping in terror. And what lay beyond it was even more chilling.

Somber Kitty leaped at May, his claws catching onto her shorts, and climbed back into his papoose.

From the sky, the flat plains beneath them had looked as if they might stretch on forever. But the view from the ground was something quite different. Up ahead, the stars disappeared, casting a long, eerie swath across the sky. The landscape—what they could see in the distance—was dark and dry, steeped in shadows and strange mounds. Beyond it, white snowy mountains rose, sending a cold mountain wind down upon the travelers and making them shiver.

The prairie—dead, dry, still, and cool—was littered with countless giant skeletons. They were lying, as if resting, and their forms were intact, though here and there a clavicle had tumbled out of place, or a spinal disk or a shoulder blade.

Sharing the landscape with the skeletons were a few enormous trees—some standing upright, some lying sideways, but all far from alive.

Beatrice drifted up to the nearest tree and tapped on it gently, then rubbed her fingers together to get off the dust and turned to look back at the others.

"Petrified," she said.

"Me too," Pumpkin moaned. "Let's turn around."

Bea shook her head. "Not petrified as in *scared*, Pumpkin. Petrified means that it's turned into stone."

May had read about places like this in one of her travel books. There was a petrified forest in the desert in Arizona. "But I thought nothing in the Ever After gets older?"

"These are older than old," Fabbio said definitively, drifting in and out of one skull's gaping mouth. He didn't even have to duck.

"Oooh, don't do that," Beatrice said, tugging his shoulder and pulling him back. "This whole place gives me a terrible feeling."

"Meay," Somber Kitty said ominously. He jumped out of his papoose, landing gracefully, and took up a protective stance beside May, facing the mountains, as if whatever danger there was lay directly ahead of them.

"Which way do we go?" Beatrice asked. Everyone looked at May.

May scanned the landscape, rubbing her arms from the chill. "Forward, I guess." Her eye lit on another stone—this one different than all the others. "Hey, look at that." They all approached it slowly, and Bea read the inscription out loud:

> *"Here lie the Frost Giants*
> *And here they stood*
> *They were believed into life*
> *And then forgotten.*
> *Now only their lonely breath*
> *Drifts upon the mountains*
> *And guards the way with fear.*
>
> *In other words,*
> *NO TRESPASSING!!*
>
> *—Signed, H. Kari Threadgoode*
> *Secretary to the Lady of North Farm."*

May touched the letters of the signed name in wonder. *H. Kari Threadgoode.*

"Sounds like their breath could be really bad," Pumpkin said. "Maybe we better not trespass."

May was already stepping past the tombstone. She turned back to look at the others. "You don't have to go."

She turned to look toward the mountains again, and then she felt Bea's arm link through hers. "I adore skeleton-strewn prairies."

May looked at her, then at Fabbio and Pumpkin as they floated up to join her. "Are you sure?"

Fabbio pulled his uniform straight and zipped ahead of her, thrusting one finger in the air. "Now we go."

May looked at Pumpkin. He straightened himself like Fabbio had, thrust a finger in the air, said, "We go," and zipped along behind him.

Somber Kitty watched the others float into the Petrified Pass. Then he looked over his shoulder uncertainly. "Meow," he said softly. Which meant, *Doesn't anyone else realize we escaped certain doom back at Risk Falls? And that it will surely follow us?*

But Pumpkin only turned around and started making kissy noises. "C'mon, Kitty. Don't be scared. They're just *bones.*"

Somber Kitty gave him a look that was meant to be sobering, but it only made Pumpkin's face bunch up in a smile. "Awww. You are sooo cute. C'mon."

Sighing, his nose wiggling for a scent in the air and his whiskers fluttering, Somber Kitty looked over his shoulder again. He supposed it was up to him alone. But what could he do?

Finally, he licked a paw and then dug it into the sand, right at the boundary of the pass. Carefully, he scraped the paw this way and that, working quickly. It was only a few moments before he sat back and looked at his creation.

He had to admit, it wasn't bad, considering his limited resources.

Minutes later, May knelt to retie her shoe just as the entire sky flashed. An enormous face appeared across the length and breadth of the sky, its eyes obscured in a tangle of leaf-shaped clouds, its pupils trained on the one tiny spot of earth where May crouched.

Only Somber Kitty happened to be looking upward at the time, and he let out a howl. But by the time the others followed his gaze, there was nothing to be seen above—nothing except layers upon layers of clouds.

Cautiously, carefully, they moved forward.

For hours May and the others made their way across the plains on a slow, steady rise that climbed closer and closer to the mountains.

Pumpkin and Somber Kitty fought to be in front, but though Pumpkin had the advantage of floating, Somber Kitty always managed to take the lead—shooting out ahead just as Pumpkin caught up again.

They were near the dislocated kneecap of a giant when May finally looked behind her. She could see the miles they'd crossed stretching out behind them, scattered with the hollow remains of giants and trees. But there was still a long stretch ahead.

"Well, how about we rest here?"

Pumpkin crossed his arms and looked toward the giant's massive skull uncertainly.

"I guess there's nowhere that isn't spooky," Beatrice said.

"This is good place," Fabbio offered, pulling a pair of binoculars out of his pocket and surveying the landscape. It was noticeably colder than it had been when they'd started out, and May blew into her cupped hands and pulled poor Kitty tight.

"Do you think if the Lady chooses, she'll just . . . zap you home?" Pumpkin asked.

"I don't know." But that was sort of what May had been thinking. Hoping. She couldn't imagine crossing the pass twice.

After they had set up camp, Bea started on a letter she planned to mail to *Coffin Confidential,* a talk show that specialized in making specters' dreams come true, sometimes uniting them with lost loved ones.

"My mom always said that when something is lost, you just have to rest your mind," May said. "And then when you least expect it, it'll come back to you."

Bea looked at her, hurt. "You think I'll never find her."

May flinched, alarm fluttering in her belly. "No, I do! I just—" It just seemed that maybe if Bea stopped pushing so hard, just for a while . . .

But Bea had already stood and, her nose in the air and her letter tucked under her arm, started floating off across the plain, leaving May watching her back, bewildered. What had she said?

That night all sorts of things kept them up. The wind howled down upon them from the north, causing May and Somber Kitty—the only two who felt the cold—to huddle together in their sleeping bag, their teeth rattling. The mountains—which again did not seem to be getting any closer—danced with strange lights, flickering here and there like lightning bugs. Even Beatrice, sleeping at a cool distance from May, had no explanation for them.

When May finally slept, she dreamed that the breeze coming down from the mountains was the breath of the Lady herself.

"Meow."

Commander Berzerko stood before the group of goblins and zombies she'd summoned. They had rendezvoused just a few minutes before, at a graveyard just north of the Dead Sea.

In her left paw she held a marker. With her right, she pointed to a collapsible blackboard, indicating a drawing she had just completed:

The commander sniffed a pawful of catnip, then surveyed the crowd. "Meow?"

The group gazed back at her blankly. Not one of the zombies or goblins present knew how to speak cat. But, since their recruitment that morning, no one had had the nerve to tell this to Commander Berzerko yet. So far they had just nodded a lot as she'd pulled out maps, done drawings, even sketched the occasional portrait.

"Meow?" the commander asked.

The zombies shifted uncomfortably. A few goblins nodded. Neither group looked at the other. Unbeknownst to the commander, zombies and goblins had been sworn enemies since 1912. (That year the goblins had determined that zombies had the worst outfits of any group of spirits in the realm.)

"Mew meow?"Commander Berzerko directed her gaze at an unfortunate goblin in the front, who'd been examining his cuticles. The goblin started and looked up in horror. Clearly aware that he was being asked a question, he pretended to be thinking really hard. He began to tremble and sweat profusely. He looked at the others helplessly. "Ufffff, meow?" he ventured.

"Meow?" Commander Berzerko considered, with deadly calm. Her eyes narrowed. And then something strange began to happen. Her fur stood up on end. Her body began to shake. Her green eyes widened and crossed. She floated several feet into the air like a balloon. All over her body, her fur formed itself into shiny black spikes. Her claws shot out into the air, smoke flowing madly from her ears. But most horrible of all was what happened to her tail.

"Meeeeeooooooooooooooow!" The tail shot out and wrapped itself around the goblin, whipping him into the air and dangling him before the others as he screeched.

And then the screeching stopped. Commander Berzerko began to shrink to normal size and float back toward the ground. Her spiraled tail unraveled itself, revealing no sign of the goblin who had been there a moment before. And then something fell from the last curl of the tail with a clatter.

A glittering black diamond.

Commander Berzerko scooped the diamond up with one paw and tucked it somewhere inside her collar as the Dark Spirits before her watched, shocked.

Calmly, she returned her attention to the blackboard and pointed once again to the figure of the cat with the big ears.

"Meow," she said. Which, though no one understood, meant, *Leave this one to me.*

May awoke to a gentle tap on her cheek. Kitty was staring at her proudly, wearing something filmy and gray. It was a little kitty coat.

Behind him, Fabbio sat with a tiny silver needle and a little sewing bag. "Now be very still, I am needing to finish hem." Noticing May staring at him, he sniffed. "What, you thinking it is unmanly to sew?" He nodded toward the white, snow-blanketed mountains in front of them. "This cat. He was not made for cold mountains." Then he muttered, "Beatrice teach me how."

May smiled. Fabbio's blue lips curled upward, his mustache curling with them. His eyes darted to the mountains. "Anyway, I no sleep."

May thought the lights must have kept him up too. And then another thought came to her. "Is this place like where you died, Captain?" she asked, pulling a petrified twig from the ground and rubbing it thoughtfully between her fingers. She knew Fabbio had died parachuting into the Alps. That was where he had lost all his men.

Fabbio stopped sewing for a moment, then nodded, his face taking on a cast as stony as the kneecap they rested against.

"Yes. . . . But was not my fault!" he added sharply, his nose going red.

"I'm sure it wasn't." May rolled her twig.

"Good morning, you two." Beatrice emerged from behind the kneecap. "Come on. I've built a fire."

May gave Bea a tentative smile, and, to her relief, Bea smiled back. It looked like she'd been forgiven.

Somber Kitty quickly glanced at the mountains, then disappeared around the kneecap in a flash.

"My sentiments exactly," May whispered.

On the third day, a light snow began to fall. By the morning of the fourth day, far up the side of one of the steepest mountains, it had whipped itself into a storm, and May couldn't see past the ends of her fingers. She, Bea, and Fabbio had to hold hands to keep from losing one another. Somber Kitty had let Pumpkin hold him for a while, pretending he didn't like it, and occasionally he peeked out of the collar of Pumpkin's coat, where he lay hidden, protected from the storm. Pumpkin drifted along happily, singing about a sepulcher in Sarasota, where his sweetheart waited for him.

"We *have* to be close to the peak," May said, pulling herself uphill by a petrified limb. She shivered under her shroud.

"What's that?" Beatrice cupped her hand over her eyes and squinted forward.

Up ahead of them, a dark hole opened up in the snow. A neon sign just at the top of it said NORTH FARM, THIS WAY.

The travelers looked at one another. A warm glow came from the tunnel.

"What do you think?" Beatrice asked.

"I think we go!" Fabbio said. "Clearly, this is shortcut."

May gazed at the opening. It seemed odd that the Petrified Pass, seemingly so forbidding, should invite them in. But May was freezing, and everyone's looks urged her forward. Even Somber Kitty had poked out of Pumpkin's coat again, his ears pointed toward the tunnel with curiosity. A tiny voice inside May said to keep trudging uphill, but she wanted to ignore it.

"Let's just go in and see," she said unsurely. The travelers hurried into the mouth of the cave.

Behind them, the neon lights flickered and then went out.

The zombies and goblins came to a stop and shivered. Ahead of them, the mountains of the Petrified Pass leaped from the horizon crookedly, sharp and menacing. Even Commander Berzerko's fur stood on end as she paced the line that separated the pass from the highlands, sniffing at where the trail of the living girl and the living cat made a straight track toward the mountains.

Now sure that the travelers had gone that way, and keenly able to scent that their trail led all the way into the mountains, she smirked, her canines poking out of her jowls.

The commander motioned a paw to the goblins, who began spreading themselves along the edge of the pass and hiding wherever they could. The zombies she sent farther east, to hide themselves in the traditional zombie style. All the exits from the pass would be covered.

Of course, it was probably unnecessary. No one who ventured into the pass ever came back out again.

The commander sank back on her haunches to watch . . . and wait.

Chapter Thirteen

Petrified, Period

In the hush of the tunnel May's and Kitty's breath furled itself across the air, drifting farther into the depths as if inviting them forward. Dripping, thawing water echoed around them. Large lumps grew out of the ground on either side of the cave, but it was hard to tell exactly what they were.

Though it was still cold, there was no wind to whip the chill into her bones, and May loosened the collar of her death shroud. She noticed it had torn in one place and that her vivid, living body showed through the tear.

"Hello?" Pumpkin called, smiling and delighted as his own voice bounced back at him. "Pumpkin is the best!" he called, cupping his long white fingers to his ears, his tuft flopping in the breeze. His echo returned again and again.

"Shhh!" May and Fabbio hissed.

Beatrice drifted up to one of the lumps, then gasped. "May, come look."

May hurried to her side.

The lump wasn't just a lump, but a statue of a ghoul—sharp fangs protruding from under its lips, its arms held up over its eyes as if in terror.

"How odd," Beatrice said.

"Maybe we shouldn't be in here," May said. But already Fabbio had drifted down the passage.

"I have found the way," he called proudly, following a glowing blue arrow on the ground. Somber Kitty leaped out of Pumpkin's coat and onto the ground, dropping back and rubbing between Pumpkin's legs.

They all reluctantly followed Fabbio. More statues emerged from the darkness: ghouls, goblins, even the occasional ghost or specter. One held a camera up to its face.

"You don't think that's one of the holo-tographers that book talked about, do you?" Beatrice whispered in May's ear. "The ones that never came back?"

May shivered.

All of the statues looked terrified. The number of them increased the farther they went, until they were practically butting up against one another.

"I think we should turn around," May said, swiveling to look back at Bea and Pumpkin. But the passage behind her was empty.

From above, the sound of a deep breath being exhaled swept through the cave, followed by a gust of frigid air.

"Pumpkin? Bea?" May whispered, then scanned the ground. "Kitty?" She shivered, and her heart thudded against her ribs. The cave seemed to have gotten about twenty degrees colder. She looked up the tunnel in the other direction, where Fabbio had drifted too far ahead to be seen.

Whhoooooooooshhhhhhh. Again, a cold gust of air swept over May and made her shiver.

"Hello?" May warbled, her pulse thrumming.

"Fabbio?" she called. There was no answer.

May strained her ears against the silence. She peered around at the different passageways, which dug their way like hollow roots outward from the open space. An icy breath from one to the right blew her hair back, her bangs parting on either side of her forehead. May walked up to the opening, pulling her shroud tight, her nose freezing. "Hello?" she called down the shaft, only to hear her echo respond.

She paused on the verge, not knowing what to do. And then she saw it. The figure was obscured by shadows, but still May could make out its thin, small form in the recesses of the tunnel.

"Hello?" she called.

Hello? her echo replied.

May crept forward, and so did the figure. It had the gait of a jaguar. Sharp, ready, poised, purposeful.

"Hello?" May squeaked again.

She paused, and so did the figure. There was something distinctly odd about it. Distinctly . . . familiar.

The figure's hair was very dark. It had glittering eyes and a thoughtful tilt to its head.

May padded up to it slowly, reaching out her hands toward her reflection in the ice. It was May, but not the May she knew. This May was older—maybe by two or three years.

She no longer had knobby knees, but long, lean, gazellelike ones. She was painted like a warrior and clothed in a dark, sparkling shroud. A quiver of silver arrows poked above her shoulder from where it hung on her back. Her hair was long, black, and lustrous and hung down along her shoulders, wild and unkempt.

"You aren't me," May whispered. This May was dazzling. She was as sparkly as the stars on her bathing suit.

May touched the mirror with one fearfully extended finger. The moment she did, she felt it was a mistake. The icy cold seemed to sear its way up her finger bone, through her whole hand, then her arm. The cold shot deeper and deeper inside her, and as it did, there was an odd stiffening in her fingers. Her body began to go rigid. She tried to pull her hand away but couldn't. May turned her head, and her neck cricked. She tried to step backward but was shocked to discover that her feet would not lift from the ground. She looked down at them. They looked . . . petrified. Like stone.

May looked up again, and the moment she did, her neck gave a crackling sound and went rigid as rock too. She could only stare at the girl in the ice, who, unexpectedly, gave her a friendly smile and a wink.

As he searched the icy cavern for May, shivering in fits despite his coat, Somber Kitty paused and sniffed the air. Something not so far away was very wrong. He had begun to wonder what it was when he was distracted, suddenly, by a figure up ahead.

Somber Kitty's fuzz stood straight up, and his tail twitched. May was up ahead, flat on her back, with a bouquet of red roses in her hands and more red roses strung about her hair. Her eyes were closed. She was lying under a glass dome, like a cake.

"Meay?" Somber Kitty whispered. He gingerly stepped up to the glass and tapped the area around her cheek with his paw. "Meay?"

This reminded him distinctly of a movie he had watched

with May when he had first come to live at White Moss Manor, on the night of May's birthday. May had cried over the television set, and Somber Kitty, then a kitten, had watched the moving picture over her shoulder: a beautiful woman with a red ribbon in her dark hair lying under a glass dome surrounded by seven little men. Bewildered, Somber Kitty hadn't understood what May was crying about, but her tears had filled him with more despair than usual. Since then he had always associated birthday cake with sadness and had never asked for scraps.

"Meay?" he asked again, tapping on the glass. May did not move. "Meay?"

Somber Kitty sniffed the glass, then sneezed.

He was slightly insulted. If this was a trick, it was a pretty paltry attempt at one. This May in front of him smelled like ice. The real May smelled like a combination of peanut butter balls, dried leaves, green grass, silver sparkles, and Ivory soap.

Bzzzzzzzzzzzzzz.

Somber Kitty turned in the direction from which the sound had come, just down one of the side tunnels. He cocked his head, wondering what on earth could have made it.

Bzzzz. Bzzzz.

Somber Kitty flapped his tail madly, wondering. The sound reminded him of a bee.

Curiosity made up approximately 45 percent of Somber Kitty's soul. And that is why, though he knew it was probably dangerous, he tramped down the tunnel to investigate.

Chapter Fourteen

Statues

*T*hunk.

The sound that came from above May was the exact same as a stopper being pulled from a bathtub. May would have flinched, had she not been made of stone. As it was, she could move only her eyeballs. But that didn't help much, because whatever it was, was directly above her head.

A beam of white-hot light, the kind she had seen only once before, poured in around her. Her heart began to pound in her frozen chest.

There was a rattle and a crunch as she felt herself being broken free of the ground at her feet, and then she was being pulled upward through the round hole that had been created in the ceiling. A moment later she was outside again, the snow blanketing the ground but no longer whipping its way through the sky.

Whatever was carrying her turned her around, and May's heart fluttered. She was surrounded by bright, white, comet-like spirits. North Farm spirits, she realized, like one she had seen in the Eternal Edifice. They parted, revealing a glowing sleigh—majestic, red as rose petals, and dripping with bells.

Inside it, leaning out at jaunty angles, were three stone statues that looked exactly like Pumpkin, Beatrice, and Fabbio.

May was carried to the red velvet bench and set down next to them. Her eyes scanned the sleigh for the one missing thing.

Somber Kitty, she tried to say, but her lips wouldn't move.

The sleigh slid into silky motion, and May tried again with all her might to open her mouth, to yell for her cat, to beg the spirits to stop. But only her pinky moved, and it moved only a millimeter. One tear of frustration squeezed itself out of her eye and down her stone cheek as the sleigh crested the rise of the tallest mountain of the Petrified Pass. And then her eyes were greeted with the view of what lay on the other side.

May, Pumpkin, Beatrice, and Fabbio beheld an enormous forest, dense with trees clinging to one another like wet herbs, the canopy of leaves dusted with a layer of snow. Squawks, squeals, and screams of wild creatures—animals!—rose up from the dark places to greet them. The smell of woods wafted into May's petrified nostrils. If her heart had not been frozen, it would have beat a different rhythm. A woods rhythm. A rhythm of home.

At the edge of the trees, just before they entered a wide, shady path, they passed a sign that said WILD AND WOOLLY NORTH FARM. The sleigh hurtled from the starlit expanse of the snowy mountain into the dark, lush greenery of the woods.

Shadows sliced across their path, made by the trees far above. Some were covered in enormous spiky briars, others were wrapped in strangler vines, and still others drooped vibrant flowers.

The trees on either side of the path seemed to bow toward

them as they passed. And from the corner of her eye, May could see vague faces in the lines of the bark, watching.

All along the path, one name seemed to be whispered through the leaves with excitement: *May Bird*.

Ahead of them, one tree rose above all the rest. Its branches curved and bent this way and that, its boat-shaped leaves were shiny and droopy and unruly, its limbs stretched out above the forest ceiling like fingers. Gigantic white flowers dripped from its branches. It was the tree May had seen all along—in the stamp on the letter she'd received back home, in the leaves above the lake, in the clouds above the City of Ether. May knew it in her petrified bones: It was the tree of the Lady of North Farm.

Other sounds closed in around them—loud crowing, rustling leaves, the buzzing of insects. The woods were alive with great translucent birds flitting here and there—birds May had seen in pictures: dodos, albatross, vultures. She glimpsed enormous Venus flytraps, glowing scarab beetles, and ferns so large that they looked like they belonged with dinosaurs. A ghostly murder of crows skimmed the air just above their heads, followed by a lone owl peering down at them. *Who? Who?* it asked.

May Bird, the trees whispered.

The sleigh turned down a path to the left and continued, away from the tree, at a thoughtful, steady float.

Several minutes passed before May noticed a plume of steam rising up ahead. When the sleigh slid to a halt, they were in front of a muddy bog dotted with round, bubbling pools.

One by one, the travelers were plucked from the seat where they were perched and dumped into the pools, with only their shoulders and heads staying above the water.

The warmth of it went straight to May's core. After a few moments she found she could wiggle one hand. Her whole body began to go warm and soft, as if she were a frozen turkey thawing. Her heart seemed to start thawing too, and every part of it that melted ached for Somber Kitty.

Glurp!

Each of the travelers was lifted gently out of the water and carried to a tiny log cabin, where they were laid on four identical beds, facedown. May felt warm, glowing hands kneading her shoulders, karate-tapping her back, pulling on her toes. Her body went as limp as chocolate pudding, and a yawn escaped from her lips.

Somewhere nearby, Pumpkin groaned. "No tomatoes. No *tomatoes!*"

May summoned the energy to swivel her neck and look in the direction of the others, lined up beside her.

Pumpkin appeared to be talking in his sleep. Fabbio's stony face was turned to her, but he still stared blankly ahead. A tiny tear dribbled a crooked line from his eye to the tip of his mustache. Beatrice lifted one hand sluggishly to her face and smoothed back a messy piece of hair.

"Purmkin," May whispered, her lips rubbery and awkward. She licked them and tried again. "Purmkin, ake up."

Pumpkin looked at her with a start. "Oh," he murmured, with a relieved smile. Then his eyes scanned the room. They widened at the sight of the North Farm spirits, but then they immediately searched the ground. Then his face grew stricken. "Where's Somber Kitty?" he whispered.

• • •

An hour or so later May and the others were all sitting up. The North Farm spirits had left them, though they could tell by the blinding light shining through the crack under the door that at least a few of them were guarding the cabin.

Pumpkin merely lay on the mud floor in despair. Great tears ran down his cheeks and froze in streaks. "I can't live without him," he cried, and rolled over to watch his tears dribble into the dirt. "I never told him how much I . . . I . . ." He broke down in sobs.

The group had curled up in a corner of the room together, huddling to warm their bones, which were still a little cold. In fact, Fabbio's big toe had not thawed in the least, and he studied it distraughtly, occasionally wiggling it with his fingers.

"What do you think they'll do with us?" Beatrice asked.

May shrugged.

They sat in silence for a long time. Finally, Fabbio broke the silence. "I have thought poem about my feelings. *Ahem.* It is called 'Ode to a Petrified Toenail,' and it go like this:

> "Once I had a lovely toe,
> but then one day it turned to stone.
> Which one, you ask? It was the pinky!
> It was my favorite toe, I think-y.
> But where there was this little toe
> There is only a shoe full of woe!
> Eeny meeny miney moe
> I will never be in a foot fashion show

> To play soccer I will never go
> To flip-flops I must say no."

Creeeeeak.

The door to the cabin creaked open, and everyone started. A spirit stood in the doorway, motioning them forward. They emerged onto a footpath and followed.

The spirit illuminated the shade and curved this way and that along the trail. Finally, a swath of dim light appeared up ahead, and they all arrived at a snow-covered pasture. A hundred paces ahead of them was another tiny cabin, smoke rising from its chimney and cobwebs clinging to its eaves.

The white spirits drifted aside, leaving the path open to the front door.

"Where are we?" Pumpkin said darkly. Bea sidled up just behind Fabbio's arm and linked her hand through the crook of his elbow.

May looked at the North Farm spirits, who watched her calmly with their slitted eyes. Everyone seemed to be waiting for her to do something. She swallowed and walked up to the door. A magnolia flower was carved into the wood.

May raised her hand to knock and then lowered it. *What if . . . ?*

There was a sudden jiggle of the knob from within, then a slow, agonized creak. The door opened.

May blinked at the two figures before her, and she almost fell over.

Somber Kitty stood on the floor, flapping his tail at her impatiently, as if to say, *What took you so long?* The other figure floated back a few inches and surveyed her with blind lidded eyes.

"The Lady doesn't live here, to answer your question," Arista said, his antennae twitching invitingly. "Zzzz. But won't you come in anyway, my dear?"

Chapter Fifteen

The Beekeeper

It was a very embarrassing spectacle for a full-grown house ghost, but Pumpkin did not seem to notice.

"Pumpkin, *zzzz*, you are not a child. Will you *please* remove yourself from my lap. Why don't you go back to hugging and kissing the cat?"

Pumpkin nibbled his fingers, but he wouldn't budge. He had planted himself on Arista, and he was not letting go. His legs swung back and forth as he bombarded his master with questions. "How's Belle Morte? How's my grave? Have you gone to the Towering Inferno Hotel without me? How're the bees? You didn't get a new house ghost, did you?"

Arista blushed. Out of a sense of decency, Fabbio picked at some lint on his uniform. Even Somber Kitty pretended to be licking his belly. They had all gathered in Arista's parlor in this new place, sitting on moldy but comfy chairs.

"Zzzzz, all in good time, Pumpkin. But surely you all have more pressing questions than these, *zzzz*. Isn't that so?"

The group stared back at him, dumbfounded.

"Zzz, well, let's see. Why don't you start by telling me what happened just now, in the Petrified Pass?"

Arista's lidded eyes were turned in Bea's direction, and his antennae pointed toward her thoughtfully.

Bea wrapped her arms around her knees. "It was frightful. Suddenly, there was no snow. We weren't even in the mountains anymore. We were in a big field, and my mother was there. She was all the way across the field, and for some reason, she was carrying two suitcases. We each saw the other, and we were about to dash toward each other, only someone else was there. Someone I couldn't see." Bea shuddered. "They took her away."

Fabbio waved a finger in the air. "I did not see this. Back there in the mountains I see my men. In the snow. I call out to them, and they see me, too. Only," Fabbio sniffed, "they run away. They call me 'Wrong Way Winky.' They say I get them lost in the Alps and that is why we all died. They strip me of these." He gestured to the shiny medals gracing his uniform, looking surprised to see them still there, then shook his head and turned his attention back to his frozen toe. "Me! *Captain* Fabbio!"

"That's nothing," Pumpkin warbled. "I ran into a group of spirits who work for the Shakespeare Song and Dance Revue. I don't know what they're doing all the way out here." He snorted sadly now and wiped his eyes. "They asked me to audition. Only . . ." Pumpkin scrunched up his eyes, unable to look at the others. "Only, when I did, they threw tomatoes at me. They said my song choice was uninspired and that I was just a two-bit, no-talent house ghost. And they said the only place I'd ever get a singing job would be on a cruise ship." He dropped his face into his hands and began to cry tears of sorrow this time. "A cruise ship!"

Something was beginning to dawn on May. "Petrified," she said.

"What?" Beatrice asked.

"I don't know." May looked at her hands.

Arista studied her closely with his blind eyelids. "What do you think happened, May?"

"We saw our worst fears. The things that most petrify us. Pumpkin's scared of failing in front of an audience." She turned to Bea. "You're scared of your mother being lost forever. Fabbio's scared that it was his fault that his men died."

Fabbio let out a big sniff. "I am 'fraid of no such thing," he said, tugging at his stone toe.

Bea patted his arm. "Of course not, Captain."

Arista nodded. "Yes, yes, precisely. Very good, dear." He leaned back in his chair. "Zzz, you're very lucky you had an invitation. The Lady dispatched the North Farm spirits to collect you, I suppose. I was down there looking for you myself, just in case, when Kitty found me."

Then everyone turned to May. They waited. May had a feeling she knew what they were waiting for, but she didn't want to acknowledge it. In fact, she pretended to be braiding her short bangs.

"What did *you* see back there?" Beatrice finally asked.

May felt her face flame up. What could she say? Herself?

"Bo Cleevil," she lied, looking at the ground. "I saw Bo Cleevil." She braided another handful of bangs, then turned to Arista. "Um, what are *you* doing here?" she asked, changing the subject.

"I received an invitation too, *zzzzz*. The day before you arrived in Belle Morte, actually."

"*Before* I arrived in Belle Morte?"

"Yes, yes. The Lady said you'd need a familiar face once you got here."

May was baffled. "You've known the Lady this whole time?"

Arista paused. "Oh, yes, dear. And, of course, we knew you would make it. Good job!"

May didn't know what to do or say. She looked at Beatrice, who was eyeing her carefully.

"I teleported up here yesterday. *Zzzzz*. Took a little less than an hour. Pleasant, really. Lovely views . . ."—he frowned thoughtfully—". . . for the most part."

A big lump had formed in May's throat. Her mind raced, putting all the pieces together. *Teleported*. Which meant, if they had known she would end up here anyway, she could have just been teleported herself.

"May, you have something to say." Arista's antennae pointed to her matter-of-factly.

"Yes." May clenched her fists at her sides. "When I was in Belle Morte," she started, stumbling a bit over her words, "you said . . . you said you didn't know *what* I should do, so I went to the Eternal Edifice, and that boy Lucius got hit with seawater, and—and—" May thrust a finger in the air. "John the Jibber! And we nearly got eaten by dogs, and then the Bogey . . ." Her voice cracked along the edge of tears. "You *knew*?"

"The Lady knows everything," Arista said calmly. "It was all for a reason."

At this May's eyes glinted like steel and her heart felt razor sharp. How could such terrible things have happened for a reason? *What* reason? Arista, it seemed, chose to ignore this. He lifted a tray of skull cakes from a nearby table and held it out to her. May took three and shoved them into her mouth. Once she was done eating, she stared at her feet for a long time. She curled her toes in and out—the same thing she used to do when she tried to do a difficult math problem at school and her brain wanted to go somewhere else. Somber Kitty leaped into her lap and curled into a ball, staring up at her sadly.

May blinked up at the ceiling to keep back her angry tears. Arista sighed. "I couldn't very well tell you, *zzzz,* could I? Meddle with your choices, *zzzzz.* Where would you be then?"

Pumpkin was now standing with his arms crossed. "I got speared by a ghoul. And I almost got turned into nothing. And I got tomatoed by imaginary spirits."

There was a long moment of silence as May tried to imagine what Arista had asked—*where she would be.* The Bogey wouldn't be after her, John the Jibber wouldn't have betrayed them, Lucius . . .

"I don't understand," she said between clenched teeth.

Arista fluffed a pillow between his hands. "*Zzzzz,* of course not. Nobody does." Arista turned to Fabbio, who was snuggling a blanket against his cheek. "Comfort blankets. Only the best here in the Far North."

"The Lady, is she a good spirit?" May asked. She wanted to add *at least?*

"Oh, I wouldn't say that. *Zzz.* She is a bit of everything, I suppose."

"But if she isn't good, then is there any hope against Bo Cleevil?"

Arista smiled, but it was a sad smile accompanied by droopy antennae. "I don't know, dear."

The group settled into a long, thick silence. Soon Fabbio began to snore.

"Arista, did you tell anybody back home that I was on a mission?" Pumpkin asked, looking respectfully somber but curious. "What did they say? They didn't believe it, right?"

Bea drifted to May's side and knelt down. "You should get some sleep."

"Oh, *zzzz,* I'm afraid that won't do," Arista said, overhearing. "I wish you could, my dear." He drifted to her as well and put his hand on her shoulder, in his first gesture of comfort. "The Lady expects you."

Out in the pasture the snow let out tiny hisses as it landed, flake by flake.

Chapter Sixteen

The Lady at the Top of the Tree

May stepped out onto the dusky, snowy path, and Arista shut the door behind them, the sound resonating across the field. With Arista drifting in the lead, they turned left and circled onto a path behind the cabin, entering the woods on the other side of the field.

Under the canopy, thousands of fireflies had sifted out of their holes to fill in the spaces between the trees. May breathed in the woodsy smell, and the forest air ran between her fingers and her toes, the way it had done when she was running wild at home.

They wound their way deep into the forest, to where the trees grew even larger and wider. The cracks in the bark were deep enough for May's fingers to fit snugly inside.

Eventually, a deep green glow appeared up ahead, and a few minutes later they came to a circular clearing punctuated by giant roots bursting through the surface of the ground. The roots emanated from a huge magnolia tree that dwarfed all the others—May was sure it was the one she'd seen from the sleigh. Her eyes slid from the base of the trunk upward in wonder. Every inch of wood was covered in glowing, green lightning bugs. Breathlessly, she scanned the limbs above for a sign of the Lady, but the upper reaches of the tree were obscured in leaves and shadows.

Though no flowers were visible from the ground, a couple of giant seedpods dangled from the lowest branches, covered in bright red seeds that clung to sticky strings of sap.

May turned to look at Arista, but he seemed unamazed by it all. His antennae twitched perkily. "*Zzzz,* this is where I leave you, dear. Good luck."

"Wait!"

Arista had already turned and, buzzing along, was drifting back down the path by which they had come. May watched him vanish around a bend in the trail, then craned her head back on her neck and looked up the tree again. She adjusted the straps of her bathing suit under her shroud, smoothed her hair, and approached the trunk. She circled around it once, then again. She looked up and around, not sure what she was supposed to do.

"Hello?" she called. Far above her, leaves rustled and scraped, but no one appeared. She waited for several minutes. There was no way to climb the tree that she could see—*if* that was what she was expected to do.

She stood there awkwardly, twirling her fingers nervously, occasionally staring up. The air got chillier, and she rubbed her arms. The woods grew darker, and the shadows began to deepen.

Rustling and whispering, the trees on the edge of the clearing leaned in curiously.

May was so busy trying to figure out what to do that she failed to notice the strange mist emerging from the tree behind her.

Mayyyyyy Birrrrd, it whispered.

May shot up, whipping around. The tree was shrouded in a mist as thin as a thread of smoke. It circled the tree once, then twice in a long, sinuous ribbon.

Mayyyyyy Birrrrd.

May stumbled back a few feet.

She could just make out two slits of eyes in the mist, then a mouth, as it circled and circled the magnolia.

"Wh-what are you?" May asked. Behind her, the other trees rustled, as if giggling.

A great breath seemed to issue from the mist like the wind, sending the dry leaves on the clearing floor scuttling. When May looked at her feet, the leaves were arranged, just vaguely, into letters.

Tree spirit, they spelled.

May gulped.

There was another wind, another rustle, and another set of leaves blew into words at her feet, so faint that if she hadn't been looking, May would never have noticed them.

H. Kari Threadgoode at your service.

May didn't know whether to gasp or laugh. That a tree spirit had been writing to her was something she'd never suspected— and that it was named H. Kari Threadgoode was almost as odd.

The leaves changed again: *The Lady is waiting.* With that, the mist swirled its way up around the tree, seeming to beckon her.

May looked at the glowing bark, covered in millions of crawling creatures. Then she shook her head. "I don't know how to get up," she called. But the mist continued to swirl upward, finally disappearing from sight.

"Wait!" May cried. At the sound of her voice, the thousands of lightning bugs covering the bark of the great magnolia took flight, surrounding her in a glowing cloud of fluttering wings. May instantly felt she had made a big mistake. The bugs began to land on her, covering every inch of her arms and legs and face. Their wings fluttered madly. May shuddered and gasped.

And then she felt her feet leave the ground.

Rising and rising, May closed her eyes tight. For a long while she felt herself going up, up, up, until her dangling feet knocked against something solid. Her whole body tickled as the thousands of lightning bugs deposited her there, unstuck themselves, and fluttered downward in a bright twitching cloud to reclaim their spots on the bark of the tree.

May was standing in a cluster of limbs gnarling their way skyward. She held on to a nearby leaf to steady herself and steeled herself to look down. As she did, she swayed. The ground was small and far away.

Up ahead, a shuffling among the branches startled her and made her grab her leaf tighter. May squinted hard, trying to make out what had caused the noise.

"Hello?" Unsteadily, and holding on for dear life, she stepped forward, out onto the limb. "Are you there?" To her left, an enormous magnolia flower clung to one of the branches. May gazed into the cup of its waxy petals in wonder as she shimmied past it slowly.

. The limb tapered, and soon there was enough room only for May's two feet and the plunging space on either side of her. More shuffling came from up ahead, and then, about ten feet away, two eyes peered at her through spaces in the leaves.

Two eyes May knew well.

They blinked at her. A cackle issued from the place where they appeared, and then they vanished.

Suddenly, the limb that was holding her began to rattle and shake. From the limb, a tiny pod sprouted large green leaves and an oval-shaped bud. May watched in amazement as the bud unfurled, not into a flower, but into a waxy white figure as fragrant as May's mother's perfume.

A hand—old and wrinkled—slowly pushed the white veil of the petals aside, revealing a small woman, as small as May, her face deeply wrinkled, her hair tangled up with moss and decaying leaves. Her dress was a cascade of twigs caked with leaves and mud. She moved her hands to her face, slowly, looking as if she were holding herself together. And then in one swift movement she crouched against the limb and disappeared.

"Here!"

May swiveled to look behind her, still swaying on the limb. The woman sat on a throne made of roses, nestled within two giant leaves. Her face white, her hair a long curtain of moss, she looked no longer decrepit, but kind and beautiful. As her blue eyes glinted, her arm shot out to steady May.

"Have I changed? Or are you just looking at me differently?"

May winced. The woman's breath smelled like the oldest apple rotted away and turned into soil, turned into roots, turned into a tree that had decayed and turned back into soil. It wasn't completely terrible, but it was full and heavy and thick.

"Are you the Lady?"

"Don't ask silly questions." The Lady leaned forward. Her

voice came out low and steady, womanly, but with a deep rumble to it. "You've come too far for that."

The two stared at each other for a long moment, the Lady taking May in with a gaze so sharp, so direct, that May felt it saw through to the pit of her soul. May waited for the wise words that were sure to pour out. Maybe the Lady was about to tell her the meaning of life or the square root of pi. She straightened her spine and listened.

"Did you have any trouble getting here?"

May was speechless. Trouble? *Any* trouble? "Um, a bit."

"Hmmm." The Lady nodded. "Tell me about it."

May didn't know quite where to begin. "Well, there was a man, John the Jibber." May swallowed. "And a boy, Lucius. And Arista and the Bogey . . ." It all bubbled up to the surface, like a scrape sometimes will when someone's there to listen to how it happened. To her own shock, May suddenly felt as if she might cry. Or lay down and fall into a deep, exhausted sleep.

"There, there," the Lady soothed, drifting down from her throne and wrapping May in her arms. Close up, she smelled like flowers blooming—sweet, soft, and new. May didn't question it but just sank into her embrace. "You've done exactly what you were supposed to do," the Lady said, "and you are exactly who you are supposed to be. But go ahead, cry anyway. Even being right is worth crying over sometimes."

May let the Lady hold her tight. She didn't want to cry at all, but two glossy homesick tears squeezed their way down her cheeks.

When the second tear had dribbled off May's chin, the Lady backed away. She was old again, worn and beaten. She seemed to be sewn together with spiderwebs. So fragile that May worried for her, as if she were more fragile than May herself. "Let's go get comfortable."

She led May under the shelter of a cluster of leaves, to a table with two chairs. Posters and old photographs covered the walls, and May couldn't help but stare.

"That's me and Methuselah," the Lady said, pointing to a photo of her and a very wrinkled man. "Me and Ishtar," she explained, hooking her thumb at another. A poster hung over the table that said I LEFT MY HEART IN BABYLON. "Lots of good times. Lots of bad times, too, but we don't take pictures of *those*, do we? Pity, really. Bad times can be beautiful, in their way."

The Lady sank into one of the chairs and rested her wrinkled chin on her wrinkled hands, staring at May, waiting. May stared back. "How's Pumpkin?" the Lady asked.

May goggled at her. This was not how she had expected things to go at all. The Lady reminded her of her granny. She cocked her head, surprised. "Um. Fine."

The Lady's eyes glinted affectionately. "He's not just your house ghost, you know. He's your guardian spirit. His soul is tied up with yours, for always. He is your protector and your ally."

May took this in. No wonder her life was so complicated. The Lady let out a deep, thick laugh. "Well?" she asked.

May goggled at her some more.

"You came to ask me something. Let's out with it."

May blinked, suddenly frightened again. "You . . . you sent me a letter. You asked me to come."

The Lady winked. "But that's not why you came."

May just stared.

"I should be more specific. You have two questions. Trust yourself enough to ask them."

May leaned back in her chair. She smoothed down her bangs nervously. "Am I really that girl, the one I read about in *The Book of the Dead*?" she muttered, surprised at the words as they came out of her mouth. It wasn't the question she'd meant to ask.

"You already know the answer to that."

May's heart gave a thud. "I'm not a fighter."

The Lady shrugged nonchalantly. "You're a hider. That's what you're thinking. And you're right."

May swallowed and nodded, feeling very small.

The Lady kneaded her wrinkled hands. "What you are hiding from the most, my dear, is that you are none of those things you are so afraid of being—cowardly, weak, small. You are a warrior of the strongest, bravest kind. You aren't afraid to *know* you're afraid. And you're *most* afraid that you're stronger than you know. I know about the girl you saw, in the caves of the Petrified Pass." She tapped her temple with a crooked finger. "You will grow into her like a hand-me-down dress. One day she will fit you just right."

The Lady gazed at May intently, as if waiting for a reply. But May could think of nothing to say.

"Sorry." The Lady waved her hand in the air. "I tend to get mysterious sometimes. Old habit. The answer is yes. You're the girl in the book. Incidentally, I *wrote* the book. And you could save the realm, possibly. That's one possible future. Also, you could end up selling skull dogs in Stabby Eye and making a good living at it, until Bo Cleevil comes, of course, and destroys Stabby Eye. Hauls you off to his fortress in the Northeast like all the others. But I don't think that's what you want. Which brings us to your second question."

Now she had changed again. She had the look of a panther: Her eyes were sharp and glinty, her fingernails seemed to be claws, her body, though old, seemed poised to pounce.

May stared at the leaf wall just beyond the Lady's right shoulder. She could feel her hands shaking. A weight of horrible guilt and fear settled over her. "Can I go home instead?"

The Lady's eyes flashed. "Of course."

May gasped. "Really?"

"Yes, if I decide to let you." She tilted her chin, staring up at May from under mossy eyebrows. "Is that what you want?"

May nodded, with a sinking feeling. "Yes."

"Yes, eh? Not 'I think'? Not 'maybe'?"

May nibbled on her pinky nail, then shook her head. "No. I want to go home."

The Lady nodded solemnly, then stared at her for a long while. "I will consider it."

May sank back in her chair breathlessly.

The Lady stood and floated around thoughtfully, as if turning over something very seriously in her mind. She gazed out from the limbs into the forest, seeming to look beyond it. "There is a third question. You won't ask it, but I'll tell you the answer. The Ever After *is* in danger. Your friends, everything. It's possible that if you go home, it won't be fixed."

"Is it possible that it will?"

The Lady thought. "I don't know." There was a long pause as they stared at each other again. "May, you don't want to fight. But sometimes, to keep what matters, you have to."

"But why? Why me?"

"May, really."

Out of nowhere, the lady pulled down a white screen from the branch above. She then disappeared, reappearing a moment later as she wheeled a shiny silver slide projector in front of May. She flipped the switch and centered the square of light on the screen.

The first scene showed a bunch of balloons May had once tried to use to fly off her mom's car. *Click.* The second slide was of the line of precious quartz rocks on May's shelf back home. *Click.* The wall of drawings in May's room, of wildly imagined places and creatures. *Click.* Somber Kitty in a golden warrior costume.

"Only you see the world the way you do. This is your gift." The Lady pointed to May's chest with one clawed finger. "You know where your heart is. When you are strong enough to hold on to that, you are strong enough to do anything. Too many people forget."

May moved her hands so that she was sitting on them. She couldn't help but hold her breath.

"You see, this"—the Lady nodded toward the screen—"is everything Bo Cleevil is not. He only wants to take. Whatever he was or has, has disappeared. He is a great big empty nothing. A thief who tries to fill himself up with things that belong to others."

May remembered the great big empty feeling she had sensed at the edge of the world. "I think I saw him," she blurted out.

Even this did not seem to surprise the Lady. "You *know,* you mean."

May thought about it. Yes. She knew.

"And you were sad for him."

May nodded, feeling foolish.

"There's no need to feel foolish for having a gentle heart."

"He said we're all just made of stardust," May murmured. "He says we're very small."

The Lady, to May's surprise, laughed at this. "And what's wrong with small?" The picture of the quartz rocks flashed back onto the screen, their surface woven with shiny white crystals. "People said all those rocks you collected were worthless," the Lady said. "You have to believe otherwise, about all the things people say, if you are going to get anywhere worth going."

"I can try."

"Oh, May. Trying is the *only* thing. Always try."

The slide show continued long into the night, and May and the Lady talked about all the images—things May had seen, the kids at school, and, finally, May's mom.

The Lady squinted, seeming to look inward. "I'm fearful for her. I can understand your wish to get back to her."

May's hands, still underneath her, had begun to go numb, but she clenched her fingers tightly together at the Lady's words. "Fearful? Why?"

But the Lady only stood abruptly, and this time she looked like a teenage girl, fresh and excited and full of energy. She led May to an enormous magnolia flower, its petals ever so slightly open, wide enough for someone just May's size to fit snugly inside.

"This is where you'll sleep."

Before she said good night, the Lady paused at the opening of the flower and looked at May. "Do you know you have known me all of your life? Do you know you recognized me in the woods? Do you know I was always calling you?"

May was dazzled. She didn't answer.

"But here you are, my girl, and you want to go home."

May stared down at her fingernails.

The Lady sighed. "Stay here tonight. I'll give you my answer in the morning."

That night May slept tucked deep inside the soft, waxy petals of the magnolia blossom, buried in the heavy, sweet smell. She curled like a seed in the oldest tree, a tiny speck in a waxy bulb in a vast forest, in a wide realm, in a universe so endless that she was only a speck on a speck on a speck, dangling in space.

Chapter Seventeen

The Letter in the Leaf

Sitting near the edge of the Pass, bored, Commander Berzerko was just about to clean her ears for the third time that evening when she noticed something curious to her left. Her tongue paused on the pad of her paw, and she stared a moment longer. Then she stood up and padded over to what had caught her eye, quickly recognizing it for what it was: a drawing in the dirt.

The commander sniffed the drawing for a second, then pulled back, licking her lips. It smelled like the living cat. But then, Commander Berzerko had always made it a point of pride that she was the only cat in the universe—with the exception of one or two artist cats she had heard of in Manhattan—who knew how to draw.

As she studied the mouse more intently, a long thread of saliva dripped from her mouth. Her gaze followed the line of the arrow. Could there really be a mouse that way? Commander Berzerko had not chased a mouse in years.

She glanced back at the Petrified Pass. The travelers would never come out anyway. And if they did, she would be able to smell them from miles away (had the mouse ventured to scurry that far) and hurry right back. In any case, the pass was covered by South Place's most fearsome slew of goblins and zombies.

Why waste the opportunity?

The demon cat floated off into the distance.

When May climbed out of her flower in the morning, she was greeted not by the Lady, but by a letter pinned to a leaf.

> *May,*
>
> *I am a busy woman, and I didn't want to wake you, as you'll need all of your rest for what lies ahead. I have decided that, yes, I will grant your request. Unfortunately, I cannot "send" you home. But I can tell you how to get there.*
>
> *You know about the four portals that lead from this world to Earth. There is a fifth almost no one knows about. You'll need to steel your courage to get there.*
>
> *You'll see a bag at your feet.*

May looked down. There was a black velvety sack resting on the limb.

It contains gifts. Some that you'll need and some that I want you to have.

You'll find new death shrouds—one for you and one for Somber Kitty. Yours may be a touch too large, but don't worry, you'll grow into it—and the nice thing is, it'll never fall off. Both shrouds will be more convincing than that rag you are toting around now. For one thing, you won't have the unmistakable smell of the living any longer.

There's a new bathing suit (I noticed yours has seen better days) and a key. You'll know when to use the key, I hope. The necklace is for your friend Beatrice. The flowers will bloom for her only if she's willing to let them. I don't think she realizes yet that the mind can't control everything. Sometimes you need to go with your gut. There's also a compass—you can guess who that's for. I'm afraid I haven't got anything for Pumpkin. Oops—it just slipped my mind. I'm sure he'll understand.

And, well, the last thing in the bag is a surprise. Maybe a good surprise, maybe not.

May, there is an enemy pursuing you that you're not expecting. Be careful.

Now, to your escape.

You've met our friend the Bogey. The way home is under his bed. I know you must be sorry to hear this. It is dangerous, yes. But no risk, no gain, is what I always say.

Good luck, May. I hope we see each other again sometime.

P.S. I know everybody is saying I am partly evil. They're right, I must admit. But don't forget, I am also very good.

The Lady had not signed her name. There was only the stamp, like the one May had seen on the letter she'd found in the Briery Swamp post office and on the telep-a-gram she'd received on the train. She knelt down and opened the bag, pulling the items out one by one.

The first thing her hand closed around was the key. May knew it just by the feel of it. But when she pulled it out, she saw it looked nothing like the key John the Jibber had used to get them into the Eternal Edifice. This key was black and luster-less, the handle shaped into a ghoulish head with a frightening pair of eyes. May studied it for a long second. Then, not want-ing to look at it any longer, she stuck it into the pocket of her shorts. There was the necklace, with one end strung through a tiny hole at the other end. A miniature living magnolia bud hung from the middle. May smiled. Beatrice would think it was beautiful.

She pulled out a black velvet garment with a hood and a cinched collar. May lifted it to herself gingerly. It was much lighter than the shroud she wore, which was by now muddy and crusted with goo and cat fuzz. May untied her old cape and laid it aside, then pulled the new one around her shoulders. She tied it at her neck and stood, surveying herself.

"Whoa!" The moment she rose, she *rose*. May's feet lifted inches off the ground. She swayed and wiggled in the air, tilting every which way, thrusting her arms out for balance.

"Wow!" She laughed and spun around, her feet fanning out beneath her. She looked down at her body, which was now just as transparent as Bea's or Fabbio's or Pumpkin's. She shuffled her feet in the air. She leaned forward and drifted effortlessly from one end of the tree limb to the other. At the very tip she stumbled forward and almost fell. May jerked backward, balanced herself, and—sobered a little—drifted back to the bag. Apparently, *floating* didn't mean she could *fly*.

She dug in the bag again, this time pulling out a much smaller cape with a little hood and ear holes. She laughed with delight.

The bathing suit came next. She peered around to make sure no one was looking, then pulled off her shorts and her old suit, yanking on the new one and pulling the straps over her shoulders. She looked down at the fabric and gasped. The sky and stars in the fabric were moving. Nebulae bursting with colors, floating clouds of cosmic dust, twinkling stars, sparkling supernovas, tiny comets shooting across the sky. Her bathing suit looked like the night sky, for real.

Grinning, May dug in again and retrieved a compass like the one Arista had given her back in Belle Morte that said RIGHT WAY, WRONG WAY, and SCENIC ROUTE. By the look of it, there was only one thing left. May was glad the surprise would come last.

She reached into the bag, and her hand closed on something cold and metal. She felt along to one end of it and felt her heart thud. She turned the bag inside out, revealing the surprise: a bow and a silver quiver full of gleaming silver arrows.

There was a tag attached to one of them: EXOR-ARROWS. THEY TURN DARK SPIRITS TO SOLID SILVER. TAKE THEM.

May stood and floated backward awkwardly, thrusting out her arms for balance. The girl in the cave had had these too. She didn't want them.

May looked at the arrows. They didn't just glint, they

gleamed. She drifted back toward the spot and touched one silver shaft—it felt cool to the touch, but her finger, once she pulled it away, went warm and tingly.

They *were* beautiful.

Slowly, May pulled one of the arrows out of the quiver. Instead of having a sharp point, it was tipped with a silver magnolia petal.

May lifted the quiver gently. She pulled the strap over her head and around her back. The arrows were as light as a feather. Strangely, they felt like they belonged.

The others were gathered in an anxious circle in Arista's living room when May returned. They all leaped out of their seats—all but Arista—when she came through the door and gaped as she floated before them.

They stared at her in silence for a few moments.

"Meay," Somber Kitty said, leaping onto her shroud and clinging to it until she lifted him into her arms. She looked around the room. Pumpkin had his fingers in his mouth, suddenly shy. Fabbio and Beatrice stared at her as if they'd never seen her before. Arista's antennae twitched excitedly.

May, confused, turned to see herself in the mirror beside the door. Her bathing suit spun with stars. She floated an inch above the ground. Her bow and arrows glinted on her back. She turned back to the others, blushing.

"Zzzz, my dear. You are—"

"Magnificent!" Bea gushed.

"I need to leave the Ever After," she said. "And I need to go to South Place to do it." She waited for a moment, her chin lifted defiantly in case they should try to talk her out of it. "I'm sorry. But I've got to go."

The group all gaped at her, then cast looks at one another.

"South Place!" Fabbio finally exclaimed, slapping his hands against the sides of his face. "And May is a sorry!"

Bea stilled him with her hand, then turned her big blue eyes on May and nodded. "We're going with you."

Chapter Eighteen

Ghouly Gum

The following morning Arista woke them all. They had stayed up late the night before, discussing their route to the Dead Sea. Arista had directed them to a town called Hocus Pocus.

"It's the gateway town for the Dead Sea," he'd explained. "They manufacture most of the stuff that's used to terrorize people on Earth. Nightmare potions and hexes and so on. Wild town. Lots of Dark Spirits coming to dance at the clubs, get their fortunes read, gamble. Occasionally, they eat someone, but nobody does much about it. They can't these days, really. *Zzz*, there's a lighthouse there—it's the entrance to South Place."

May quickly shot a glance at Pumpkin, who was still hunched over his elbows, sulking because he hadn't gotten a present from the Lady.

"*Zzz*, to get to the realm below, Dark Spirits can simply *jump* into the water. But for anyone else, jumping in zaps you straight to the Dungeons of Abandoned Hope." Arista shivered. "Or so I hear. *Zzzz*. Far better to use the door. Of course, I hope you don't run into anything, *zzz*, unsightly on the stairs."

Arista opened the curtains to let in the starlight. "*Zzzz*, time to get started. Better to get as far as you can before the Dark Spirits get wind you'll be going this way. They'll be looking for you. *Zzz.* Be sure to keep your destination under your hat." His antennae twitched toward Pumpkin in particular. "Unless you want a greeting party waiting for you when you get there. *Zzz.*"

When everyone had packed their things, Arista drifted to the front door. "I have something for you." He ushered them outside, where everyone let out sighs of amazement. Four glowing horses floated in a line outside the door.

"They won't take you far—they're banished from the rest of the realm, as you know. *Zzzz.* But they'll get you to the edge of the pass at least."

There was a gentle white horse for Bea. A regimental horse in braids and ribbons for Fabbio. A speckled pinto for Pumpkin. The only horse left was a huge black stallion in silver reins, with a pouch hanging off the side for Somber Kitty. "I suppose that's yours, May," Beatrice said.

Pumpkin bear-hugged Arista, his gangly limbs flailing. "Thank you, thank you, thank you!" He then ran up to his horse and threw his arms around its neck.

Sometime later, after a tearful good-bye, the weary group set out into the cold.

Hours afterward only Pumpkin had perked up, rocking back and forth on his horse and singing: *"Ohhhhh, a horse is a horse, of course, of course, and no one has one in the realm, of course, unless that horse is a spirit horse named Pumpkin Is the Bessssst!"*

"I can't believe you named your horse Pumpkin Is the Best," May mused with a sardonic smile, shivering.

Fabbio held up his new compass for the thirtieth time that morning. "We are all accounted for," he said. "Heading the Right Way."

Nobody made one complaint, but May knew what they must be feeling. They had come all this way with hope of rest. And here they were, on a path more dangerous than ever.

The group wended its way out of the valley along the east side. They drifted along the lowest rise of the snowy mountains and climbed steadily, May and Kitty snuggling together for warmth.

When they crested the mountain, they took a break. On one side they could see the green, lush forest of North Farm. On the other there was the unmistakable, permanent dusk of the Ever After, a vast empty plain crisscrossed above by shooting stars. May looked back toward the Lady's tree. She gave a little wave but could not tell if anyone was watching.

They decided to camp there for the night. Somber Kitty, enchanted with his custom death shroud, chased his transparent tail, zipping between May's hovering feet and executing the occasional flip. Pumpkin, Bea, and Fabbio said very little, staring at one another somberly. Without having to ask, May knew they were thinking about the same thing: South Place.

The next morning they left as soon as May and Kitty woke. Even on the east side of the Petrified Pass, the bones of the ancient giants were strewn everywhere. The group did not slow until they were approaching the edge of the pass.

"The Nothing Platte," Beatrice said, scanning the view of the empty flatness in front of them, punctuated only by the giant bones that lay just outside the very edges of the pass. "There isn't anything for miles now but the Scrap Mountains. It's a wasteland."

Fabbio held his compass aloft, proudly, clearly convinced that the Lady's gift confirmed he was the group's trusted navigator and captain.

May, on the other hand, was distracted. She had the uneasy feeling that something wasn't right.

"We go," Fabbio said, climbing down from his horse. The others followed. Only Pumpkin remained on his mount, laying flat on his stomach and holding him tight about the neck, staring at May pitifully, his bottom lip stuck out.

"Pumpkin, we have to let them go," May said, reaching up to pat his arm.

Pumpkin flipped his head so it was facing the other way. His tuft of yellow hair waved at May defiantly. "No."

"Pumpkin," May said more sternly. "You need to get down this instant."

"No."

May looked back at Captain Fabbio and Bea, who shrugged helplessly.

"Pumpkin, maybe Captain Fabbio will let you hold his compass for a while if you come down." She sent a pleading look back at Fabbio, who clutched his compass to his chest protectively. Then, shooting a look at Pumpkin, he softened.

"It's a very shiny, Punkin," the captain said enticingly.

Slowly, and with great, loud sniffles, Pumpkin slid off Pumpkin Is the Best. He held out his long bony fingers for the compass.

Once the horses had gone, the group continued forward out of the pass, coming to the last set of giant bones—two enormous skeletons with their hands outstretched to each other.

Pumpkin drifted into the space between the enormous fingers. "It's creepy here." He frowned, turning toward May. "Do we really have to go to Hocus Pocus?"

"Shhh!" everyone hissed at once.

"What?" Pumpkin looked around.

"Arista said to keep that quiet, about Hocus Pocus."

Pumpkin looked back and forth. "There's nobody here."

Just then a little black blob emerged from behind one of the giant bones. Everyone froze.

"Is another cat?" Fabbio whispered.

"Mew," Somber Kitty said, insulted.

Upon closer inspection, the blob looked like a goblin, only sort of friendly. It was smiling at them widely with its razor-sharp teeth. It reached into the pocket of its gabardine skirt and pulled out what appeared to be a pack of Ghouly Gum, offering it to them. Everybody drifted backward except for Pumpkin.

"Oh," Pumpkin said, staring at the gum, clearly torn. It even had a shiny wrapper. He looked at May, who shook her head furiously, then he nibbled on his fingers and looked back at the goblin. "Well, I don't mind if I do."

Pumpkin squatted and took the gum. "Thanks." He smiled companionably at the goblin, who smiled back, wider than ever. Pumpkin unwrapped the gum and put it in his mouth. Chewing, he let out a sigh of satisfaction and looked back to the others as if to say, *See?*

And then the creature smiled even wider, opened its mouth, and tried to bite off Pumpkin's arm.

"Ahhhhhhhhhhhhhhhhhhhhhh!"

As if on signal, a score of goblins leaped out from behind the bones and onto Pumpkin. *"Ahhhhh!"* Pumpkin's mouth spread into a huge, crooked, screaming O as he zipped ahead, trying to shake them off as they dangled from his shoulders, his shirt. One held the puff of his hair as if it were a pair of reins.

Pumpkin zigzagged toward May and the others, waving his arms in the air and screaming furiously, "Help! Help meeee!" With a thud, he knocked into Fabbio, sending him sprawling.

Like fleas, a few of the goblins hurled themselves at Fabbio's knees while three more leaped straight for his shoulders and grabbed his military medals, trying to pry them off.

"Helllppppp!" Bea called, just as a gaggle of goblins leaped onto her dress and untied her sash. She swatted at them with one hand as she rummaged in her backpack with the other, yanking out the large, thick, dusty book on Dark Spirits. She waved it at the goblins, knocking them off of her dress. May started toward her, but Pumpkin crossed between them, three creatures dangling from his legs, trying to tie him with a long rope. The two on his shoulders jumped off and scurried toward May. Hissing and spitting, Kitty leaped before her and reared his claws.

It was at that moment that May remembered her bow and fumbled over her shoulder for it. Her arrows went clattering out of the quiver onto the ground. She swooped downward and grabbed one, stringing it, her hands shaking as if they'd been electrified. She aimed first at the goblin tugging at the bottom of

Bea's skirt. Then at the one dangling from Pumpkin's hair. Back and forth, back and forth. Finally, she chose her target and, holding her breath, let her arrow fly. The arrow gently soared into the air, poised there for a moment, and then drifted to the ground like a feather.

"Mama mia!" Fabbio howled, waving his sword from the ground as two goblins tied a length of rope around his feet in a nice bow. "What those arrows are made of? Spaghetti?!"

Bea, who'd been tripped and now sat on the ground scooting backward, flipped madly through her book, occasionally using it as a weapon. "Goblins, goblins," she muttered as she fanned the pages madly.

May swallowed and gathered her wits, grabbed another arrow, and shot it. Again, it merely sailed into the air gently, then fluttered to the ground.

She stared helplessly at the wilted arrow, then at the chaos around her.

"May, do something!" Pumpkin screamed, zigging past her. Somber Kitty had backed up almost against her ankles, fending off the two creatures in front of them.

May thought frantically. For some reason, John the Jibber came to mind.

She looked to Beatrice, who was rolling across the dust in a goblin headlock. Fabbio was groaning as two others pulled on his mustache. And Pumpkin had made his way onto the top of one of the giant skulls, trying to shake himself loose.

Suddenly, May realized why she had thought of John the Jibber. It was something he'd told her once, about goblins. She hesitated for just a moment or two. And then she cleared her throat.

"How do you solve a problem like Mariiiiiiia?" she sang, then paused, nibbling a nail.

Fabbio, who seemed to have forgotten completely that he was being hog-tied by goblins, stared frozen, his mouth hanging open in a long oval under his tortured mustache.

But the goblins, too, paused. They looked interested, but slightly disgusted.

May continued to warble, her voice coming out squeaky and off-key.

The goblins shook their heads and went back to what they were doing. One of them leaped past Kitty and grabbed May by the foot.

"How do you catch a cloud and pin it dowwwwwwn?"

Everyone stopped. This time they all turned toward Pumpkin. He was standing on the skull, looking at May unsurely. She nodded urgently, and he continued singing.

Several sighs were heard from the goblins. One sigh even escaped from Somber Kitty's lips. A couple of goblins dropped from Pumpkin's shoulders and gazed up at him raptly.

Pumpkin continued to sing the song, meeting May's eyes. When May smiled at him, his own smile grew wide. He thrust his arms into the air operatically and began to really belt it out.

One by one, the goblins let go of their captives and hobbled onto the ground. As they did, some dabbed at the corners of their eyes. They began to sidle up to one another shyly, then, slowly, they wrapped their arms around one another and hummed along. Some muttered things the travelers didn't understand. But if they had, they would have heard statements along the lines of "I have always loved those shoes" and "Lavender really *is* your color."

"How do you solve a problem like Maria?" May joined in softly.

"Meoooooooo," Somber Kitty crooned, low. Beatrice added a slight foot shuffle, and everyone followed suit.

The goblins began to sit and sway their heads back and forth, snuggling together, some wiggling their toes in the air, humming along. When Pumpkin finished, they began to look restless again. He glanced at May for guidance.

"Another," she whispered.

He nodded. *"Climb evvvery mountain . . ."*

Seven songs later (including two more from *The Sound of Music* and three from *Cats*), the goblins had passed out from exhaustion after all the excitement. When the last goblin began to snore, the group looked at one another. And then, very quietly, they tiptoed away.

Chapter Nineteen

Walk of the Zombies

Pumpkin, you were terrific!" Bea gushed.

"I know."

"Little May," Fabbio added. "Singing. Brilliant!"

They all remembered very well now the goblins they had seen in the Eternal Edifice and how John the Jibber had informed them that there was nothing a goblin loved more than a musical—except, perhaps, shopping.

As the group drifted across the Nothing Platte, they wove their way around the junk that dotted the landscape: old slurpy soda machines, worm-eaten billboards, broken-down carriages, abandoned caskets, toasters. To May, the Nothing Platte was hardly what it sounded like. It seemed to be full of *everything* the rest of the Ever After didn't want.

May walked quietly along behind the others, her thin shoulders drooping. She was happy that they had escaped and proud of her friends. But she was bewildered by what had happened with her silver arrows.

The rest of the group was still busy congratulating themselves when they crossed into the section of the platte that ran a jagged swath through the middle of the Scrap Mountains.

On either side of them, the mountains rose up lopsidedly. May could just make out the giant mounds of old hearses, broken skull-o-phones and holo-visions that lay up ahead. Already, even this far away from the Scrap Mountains, the air smelled like garbage.

Pumpkin had started to float along with his chest thrust out, transported by a wave of conceit. Every time Fabbio or Beatrice complimented him, he turned around, looking careless, and blew them a kiss. "It was nothing. Nothing," he said as he drifted on ahead.

Even Somber Kitty drifted behind him happily, in awe.

Pumpkin's head was held so high that he had no view of the ground beneath his feet. If he had, he may have noticed that it was beginning to break apart.

"Ahhhhhhhh!!"

A form rose out of the ground, sand-colored, with long matted hair and sagging features. Its empty black eyes rested dully on them. Its arms stretched out stiffly in front of it. Within moments, several other creatures had burst out of the dirt, surrounding the travelers. They were all chanting, *"Eugghhhhhhhhh!"*

May looked to Beatrice questioningly. Beatrice grabbed her hand. "Zombies!"

The zombies lurched slowly toward them.

"Run!"

They ducked and zipped their way out of the circle, Pumpkin shooting way out ahead—right into another zombie just rising from the ground. Pumpkin sprawled backward. Slowly but menacingly, his attacker bent toward him with rigidly outstretched arms.

"Mayyyy!" Pumpkin yelled, covering his eyes. Just in time, May and Beatrice grabbed him by the armpits and dragged him sideways, dodging the zombie's mechanical movements and racing ahead. Fabbio drifted up behind them, turning to float backward while he waved his sword.

They zigged. They zagged. Everywhere they turned, another zombie popped out of the ground beneath them, sending them screaming and racing in another direction.

Dodging the trash that littered the sand, they looked over their shoulders. The zombies trailed farther and farther behind, but they kept coming relentlessly.

"How do we stop them?" May yelled to Beatrice.

Bea only shook her head furiously. "Zombies are slow . . . never stop!"

Up ahead of them, Pumpkin tripped over something and went tumbling forward. May, Bea, and Fabbio skidded to a halt just before they tripped too. Between them lay what appeared to be an abandoned hearse, half buried in the sand.

May looked over her shoulder. Not far off, they could hear the zombies moaning, but for the moment they were obscured from sight by the scattered mounds of trash. May grabbed the latch on the hearse and pulled. "Help me with this!"

Everyone looked at her as if her brain had been stolen by zombies, but still, they gathered and gave a collective yank on the handle of the trunk, sending it flying open. "Get in! Get in!" May waved her arms wildly. They climbed into the dark, wide trunk, May last of all. When they were all in, she pulled the latch closed. In the darkness they hunched together. Somber Kitty leaped onto May's lap and curled into a ball.

Pumpkin tried to do the same and had to be content perching on her knee, which was exceedingly uncomfortable. The only sound was that of Somber Kitty and May breathing, their warm breath filling up the cool air inside the trunk and making it stuffy. They listened for the zombies.

"Euuuuuuuuuuggggggggggghhhhhhhhh!" Thud, thud, thud.

May felt even breathing was too dangerous, so she held her breath and pinched Kitty's nose. In the dark his green eyes glinted at her quizzically, but he did not resist.

Thud, thud, thud.

It sounded like the zombies were right on top of them. Pumpkin shifted in his seat, whimpering. A second or two more . . .

And then May heard it.

Breathing.

Someone in the trunk was breathing. And it wasn't her. And it wasn't Kitty. And ghosts didn't breathe. . . .

"Pumpkin, stop squeezing me so hard," Beatrice whispered.

"I'm not doing anything," Pumpkin whispered back.

"Smells like Uncle Bonino's pasta fagioli in here," Fabbio hissed.

It was true. Someone in the trunk had very bad breath.

At that moment the back of the trunk seemed to drop out behind them, and with a collective scream, they were all yanked backward.

Chapter Twenty

The Colony of the Undead

There was a loud shuffling sound, then the thudding of what sounded like many footsteps, and then a pause. May and the others found themselves bound together tightly by a net of old, dusty ropes. Whoever had captured them was still breathing loudly in the dark, filling the air with the stench of garlic.

The thud of zombie feet moved above them.

"You led 'em straight to us!" a husky voice grumbled. There was something familiar about it, and then May realized what it was: The accent was southern.

The captives stayed quiet, more out of fear of the zombies above than out of hope that the predicament they were now in was any better. They strained their ears.

Slowly, surely, the zombies seemed to start thudding away.

"Well, phew!"

Their captor began dragging them through the darkness, grunting with the effort and occasionally muttering to itself, until they emerged into a large, starlit cavern, walled completely with junk: crushed-up toasters and billboards and automobiles packed like sardines, forming walls and a high domed ceiling.

A greeting, cobbled together from various old signs, hung from a fender in the wall: YOU HAVE ENTERED THE COLONY OF THE UNDEAD.

"Meow?" Somber Kitty said doubtfully.

Out of the halls from all around them emerged several—maybe forty or so—spirits, all dressed in black, with powder white skeleton faces. Their backs were strapped with spears and tiny net sacks of what looked to May like onyx and silver, and bouquets of periwinkles were pinned at their waists.

"I've never come across spirits like these in my reading," Bea whispered to May as they sat shivering in their net.

"I got these here spirits runnin' from some zombies," their captor announced. "Almost led them right to us. And, look, they got a cat!"

There were whispers and mutters from the skeleton spirits, and then with one quick, sharp movement, their captor reached into the dark folds of its clothes and whipped out a gleaming dagger.

Whoosh. The knife sliced through the air and the net fell aside, and May, Pumpkin, Bea, Fabbio, and Kitty came tumbling out.

A sharp intake of breath issued from some of those spirits in the crowd.

"It's her," someone hissed.

"Who?"

The skeletal figure closest to May leaned forward and yanked back her death shroud with a flourish. The figures let out grunts and sighs of amazement, and then applause rippled over the group, faint at first, then louder. Several fell to one knee and bowed their heads. May swept Kitty into her arms. Pumpkin grinned and took a small bow, patting his tuft.

Their captor pulled off its cloak, immediately followed by its mask.

Now it was May's turn to gasp. The face was colorful, solid, flushed, and breathing. It was pudgy and round, with sly, deep-set gray eyes that matched the halo of wiry gray hair. And it was *alive*.

As if on cue, all the other figures pulled off their masks and hoods too. They were all alive!

May and her friends were speechless.

Their captor turned to a woman in flight goggles and a jumpsuit. "Amelia, go check the hearse entrance and make sure it's closed. Elvis, Jimmy, go to the lookout and find out which way the zombies are headed."

The three went scurrying off down different, junk-walled tunnels.

"What?" May asked, incredulous. "How?"

The woman turned to her, studied her sharply, and then put her hands on her hips. "Why, we're the undead, honey," she said. "I'm Bertha." She took May's hand and bowed. "Bertha Brettwaller. It's an honor to meet you."

May blinked at her, recognizing the name instantly, too stunned to reply. *The* Bertha Brettwaller? Of Briery Swamp?

"And I hear," Bertha continued, "that you're going to save us all."

Everyone sat at an old picnic table, the Live Ones arguing over who would get to hold Somber Kitty next, as May and Bertha determined that, indeed, they shared the same home in Briery

Swamp, though in different eras. Bertha hadn't seen the broad-side of White Moss Manor since 1897.

"But how are you still alive?" May wanted to know.

Though her face drooped like melting ice cream and crow's feet crept out from the corners of her eyes, Bertha talked animatedly, her puffy gray hair wild and wiry. "Oh, honey, haven't you noticed? You never get older here. We're running on star time, of course. Kind of warps things, you swannee?"

May didn't know what "swannee" meant. But it did seem that she hadn't grown even a centimeter since she'd fallen into the lake. Her toes weren't poking against her shoes. Her bobbed hair was no longer. And how long had she been here? How long had her mom been missing her?

At Bertha's prodding, May told her more about the Briery Swamp of today. Bertha was delighted to hear that her library in White Moss Manor was still intact and that the house was loved and cared for, though May wasn't able to tell her whether or not wild garlic still grew in the woods. Bertha's eyes widened at the tales of electric toothbrushes, inground swimming pools, and astronauts.

She slapped her knee and let out a husky howl of a laugh. "People on the *moon*! You don't say! Won't be long before they find us up here in the Afterlife, I reckon!"

May grinned, thinking of living people arriving in the Ever After amid the spirits and ghosts.

"How'd *you* end up here?" May inquired.

"Oh, that old water demon." Bertha let out a wistful sigh so smelly that it made May's eyes cross.

"I bet you wish we had that Ghouly Gum," Pumpkin whispered into May's ear. May elbowed him in the arm.

Bertha stretched her way into her story. It sounded as if she'd told it a hundred times before, and each time it became more interesting to her than the last. "I'm out foraging, and I find this lake, beyond the tangle of briars. You know the one I'm talking about, honey. Well, I was never a swimmer anyway. So the demon appears, looking all pretty at first—you've seen how she does." May nodded. "Well, I look over thinking I'm looking at an angel, and then *slap!*" Bertha clapped her hand on the table, making Somber Kitty do an aerial somersault off the lap where he'd been sitting. "She pulls me in. You'd think I was a goner for sure. Except suddenly, I'm getting spit up onto the shore. Only it's the *wrong* shore." Bertha leaned in ominously. "Honey, it was the *dead* shore."

May tried to cover her nose casually.

Bertha straightened up and sniffed. "Dunno why the demon spat me up like that. I reckon I taste as good as anyone else. Wouldn't you reckon, handsome?" She winked at Fabbio, grinning to reveal her garlic-encrusted teeth. Fabbio shuddered, twirled his mustache, and pretended to be studying the ceiling.

After May had filled Bertha and the others in on the changes to Briery Swamp and to Earth in general, Bertha filled her in on the undead.

"One way or another, we all ended up in the Afterlife by accident. Amelia got lost over the ocean in her plane." She nodded her head toward the woman in the flight suit, then thumbed at another in a cancan skirt, red bustier, and high-heeled black boots. "Lawless Lexy here was a knife thrower for the traveling circus. Fell into the Bermuda Triangle on her way to Indonesia. Fought her way past the water demon. . . . Plucky."

May nodded. She knew the Bermuda Triangle was one of the four doorways between Earth and the Afterlife.

"But look at me, will ya? Running on and on. I reckon everybody has things they want to ask you." She turned over her shoulder, to where the colonists perched on various stools and benches, listening to every word. Now they all scrambled to talk to May at once.

"Do you really breathe fire?" one man in a business suit asked.

"I heard you ride Black Shuck dogs bareback."

"Didn't you throw the Bogey out of the Eternal Edifice with your bare hands?"

"How do you plan to get Bo Cleevil?"

"All right now, cool your muffins," Bertha said, looking around sternly. "This girl's just had a long journey. Don't everybody hog her at once." She eyed May. "Maybe we should just take a little walk first, get you acclimatized. Whaddya think? How 'bout a tour?"

Pumpkin and May looked at each other across the table excitedly. "Sure," May replied. While the others rested, Bertha led May, Kitty, and Pumpkin through a vast network of tunnels winding their way up inside the Scrap Mountains.

"Spirits think it's just a solid pile of junk, but we been hollowing out the inside for years. Making a place of our own, where no one won't blow their Bogey whistle on us."

As they pushed through doorways made of car parts, soda cans full of old rusty nails announced their arrival. Everywhere, ropes suspended from the ceiling dangled potbellied stoves, refrigerators, large rocks, even chandeliers. "In case we get intruded," Bertha said, nodding to the precariously hung items. "You can bet how happy the baddies would be to catch a pile of Live Ones like us. That's why I had to net you. . . . Careful." Bertha dodged levers sticking out of the walls and stepped over tiny strings that crossed the walkway, guiding the others along behind her to avoid the booby traps. "You get to know it like the back of your hand, eventually," she assured them.

Bertha led them upward through one garbage-walled corridor after another, along bridges made from abandoned shackles that could be unhooked at a moment's notice, sending their occupants into the crevices below. Deeper inside, there were large cavernlike areas stockpiled with food, bars of silver, and onyx. "Helps to ward off spirits," Bertha said. "But I'm sure you know all that."

One enormous room had shelves up to the ceiling, packed to the gills with books, many of the jackets ripped off, none of them showing titles till you looked right at them and the letters drifted into view. "We get these at half price from Crawl-Mart."

Bertha turned to a stack to the right and pulled a few volumes off the shelf: *I Was a Teenage Goblin*, *Potty Training Your Black Shuck Hound Puppy*, *So You Want to Be an Evil Ruler*. She showed the books to May, then reshelved them.

"Pays to know the enemy," Bertha breathed at Pumpkin, who winced and swayed as if he might faint.

Other rooms had no ceilings but were exposed completely to the stars above, and, to May's shock, gardens brimming with vegetables, fruits, and flowers grew inside.

Bertha explained, "Got the seeds from a guy called O'Harris.

A botanist, wouldn't you know? Went down with his ship in the triangle. Lucky day for us, I reckon. We gotta live on something. We can't count on food sacrifices these days. So many people on Earth have stopped doing that kind of thing, because they've stopped believing in ghosts and spirits. Only believe in what they can see. Think ghosts are just in stories. What a bunch of ninnies." She shook her head. "*Tsk-tsk-tsk.* We can only count on ourselves now."

Bertha turned to another door. "Here's the bank." On a table sat stacks upon stacks of shining coins. "All the tele-tokens we'll ever need," Bertha continued. "We got our own teleporter so we can transport ourselves to any booth in the realm, at any time."

May gasped. "Was it you? Were you the ones who took all the tele-tokens? I saw that in the newspaper!"

A proud grin crept diagonally across Bertha's face. "You saw that too, huh? We keep a copy of every single newspaper in the archives, if you want to look at it again. We got Live Ones hidden all over the realm, honey, fighting for the cause. We got all these little ways to stick it to the big guy, even though we never even seen him. And now we got you. We knew about that whole Eternal Edifice fiasco before the Bogey was done peeling himself off the sand. Some ghouls leaked the news about *The Book of the Dead* and what it said about you. I plumb just about fell over when I heard. Ha!" Bertha patted her gray puff of hair as they made their way up, up, up, until they reached a circular door in the ceiling, made out of a hubcap.

"This is my favorite," she said, giving the hubcap a shove. It flipped open to reveal a ladder. Bertha started climbing up it and motioned the others to follow.

They emerged into the night air—and to a breathtaking sight. Half of the Ever After lay stretched out before them. They could see clear to the Dead Sea. There, indeed, was the dark lighthouse of Hocus Pocus. Dark clouds swirled above it, filling May with dread.

Pumpkin gripped May's hand. She looked back at him gratefully.

"Meow."

May directed her gaze at Kitty, who was looking at her bathing suit. Its zipping stars and supernovas caught the light and reflected it in tiny bursts, though the bursts of lightning they could see must have been miles and miles away.

"It's a great location, huh?" Bertha gushed. "It's so isolated that hardly anybody comes up here sniffing around. And we can just teleport down to the shore towns to spy on the Dark Spirits when we get a hankerin'. We been needing to do that a lot lately. They been on the move. Something big on the horizon. You can just feel it."

May scanned the view nervously, then looked at Bertha. "What are you going to do?"

Bertha shrugged. "What are *we* gonna do? Something. Anything. When we started hearing about you, our spirits rose." Bertha seemed to get choked up, but it turned out she was just wincing from a bit of garlic pricking the inside of her cheek. She stuck a finger in her mouth and moved it to where she could suck on it. "A girl who can fly outta the Eternal Edifice is sure someone we gotta have on our side, book or no book." She looked May up and down, sizing her up. "I wouldn't have thought you'd be so tiny, though. You look like a feather could knock you over."

"Bertha . . . ," May began.

"Come on," Bertha interrupted, leading them back down the ladder. "There's more."

Bertha was all business as she directed them down the next set of corridors. "How'd *you* manage to get through the portal, Miss May Bird?" she asked.

"Um . . ."

"It was mostly thanks to me," Pumpkin replied, stifling a fake yawn and looking to see if Bertha was impressed. But she already seemed distracted.

"We offer lots of classes," Bertha said, tapping her finger to her chin, hobbling ahead purposefully as she waved at this and that cavern full of neatly lined desks. A chalkboard hung on one of the hallway walls, announcing the classes scheduled for that day:

Cleevilology: 9:00 a.m.
Combat with Ultimate Evil: 12:00
Coping with Life When Everyone Around You Is Dead: 1:00 p.m.
Ready, Set, Exorcise! 2:00 p.m.

"Of course, we spend most of our time training, getting ready for the day when it's time to go up against Bo Cleevil for good."

Bertha entered one of the cave classrooms, pulled a newspaper off a shelf, and flipped to the back. "We been running an ad ever since we got the reports about you coming out of Ether." She flattened the paper against a desk, pointing to a passage about halfway down the last page. SPIRITS TOTALLY AGAINST REALM DOMINATION, the headline read. Her breath bounced off the desk and flooded May's nostrils. "We were hopin' you'd lead us to our goal."

May gazed at the words on the page. "How many of you are there?"

Bertha calculated quickly, counting on her fingers. "About forty here, and we're in contact with about ten more through the mail. Oh, and telep-a-grams. We smuggled a booth from Hocus Pocus. Between the telep-a-booth and the teleporter, we got things covered." She winked. "Anyway, about fifty alto-gether. Though we're sure there are a lot of other Live Ones in the realm who just don't know where to find us."

May thought back to the globe she had seen in Arista's study back in Belle Morte, which had listed the various populations in the Ever After. "But the Dark Spirits. There are so many. . . ."

Bertha nodded. "Plus, Bo Cleevil is probably worth about a thousand of them put together. And, of course, there's the Bogey."

May felt a lump in her throat, but Bertha tilted her chin up. "What we got in our favor is that they're still pretty scattered, those Dark Spirits. They control most of the City of Ether, that's certain. For a while they were just kinda layin' low. Like I said, though, things have picked up. The ghouls've been raid-ing towns and remaking 'em into what they call Cleevilvilles. That's cause Cleevil likes to have everything just so, you swan-nee. Everything orderly. Kinda clean and dull. And everything named after him, of course." Her gray eyes twitched with dis-dain.

She led them into the hallway again, right past the recreation hall, where Fabbio had dug out a pack of cards

and was playing a game of Old Hag with himself while
Beatrice was flipping through a book. "Pumpkin, you can stay
here with the cat. C'mon, May."

She led May to another doorway and stepped inside. "Here's
our archery range." She nodded to a figure across the range. It
was a cardboard cutout of a ghoul with snarling teeth. Somebody had drawn cross-eyes over where his real eyes had been
and a curled mustache under his snout. They had scrawled
Ghouls smell! across his chest.

Bertha studied May, her eyes drifting to her quiver of arrows.
"I wonder if I could see them arrows?"

May pulled her bow and quiver from her back and held
them out.

Bertha pulled the string taut, shutting one eye tight. "This
one's special. A real beaut. A North Farm original, I'll swannee.
Very rare."

"It doesn't work very well," May said, quietly.

Bertha looked at her askance, then handed the bow back.
"There's your target." She nodded toward the ghoul.

"Oh, I don't know," May murmured.

"It's a ghoul! You've got to do it." Bertha held the quiver of
arrows out to her. She gave May that look again, like she was
daring her.

Obediently, May took the bow, strung an arrow, drew it
back, aimed—then let it go.

Instead of soaring toward the target, or even across the
range, the arrow drifted through the air like a feather once
again, making it only a few feet before landing gently on the
ground, as if it had fallen fast asleep.

May looked at Bertha Brettwaller, and Bertha Brettwaller looked at May.

"Try again."

May tried. Again, the arrow drifted to the ground, lifeless.

"There's nothing wrong with them arrows," Bertha said. "The problem is with you. Your heart's not in it." She studied May for a long, long moment. "Otherwise, they'd fly straight."

Bertha chewed on her lips for a moment, one eyebrow descending over one eye. "You ain't planning to help us, are ya?"

May's face heated up desperately. The only thing she could think to say in response was, "I have a mom."

Bertha stared at her for another long moment.

May felt the need to say more. "The Lady says the way back to Briery Swamp is under the Bogey's bed."

Bertha was silent for a few moments more as she sucked on her garlic clove, moving it around in her mouth, ruminating. "Well, we'll take you," she finally said.

It was the last thing May had expected to hear. "Why?"

Bertha leaned forward, resting her elbows on her knees. "Well, shoot. I know what you left behind." She looked at May again, seriously, and a hundred years of sadness seemed to shine there behind her eyes. Then she smiled her garlicky smile. "But I also got a better reason."

"What's that?"

"We need you. So I've gotta believe in you."

May stared at Bertha with a heavy lump in her throat, but Bertha only stared back at her evenly, clasping her hands together. "I believe you'll come back."

• • •

Zombies, fortunately, are the stupidest of all the Dark Spirits, even stupider than ghouls, who have an IQ of –36. So when May and the others vanished into the trunk of the hearse, the zombies were left discombobulated and lost, staggering back and forth across the Nothing Platte.

Eventually, they bumped into the goblins, who were making the slow journey home, show tunes still ringing in their ears.

When the two groups converged and saw that neither of them had captured their prey, they argued bitterly. The goblins blamed the zombies, saying they wouldn't know a Live One if it bit them on the severed limb. The zombies countered this with a resentful *"Eeeeeuuuuugh,"* which was the only word in the zombie vocabulary.

And then, although they were headed to the exact same place, the two groups went their separate ways.

As the goblins made their slow way south, choosing the route with the best malls, the story of Pumpkin's singing went with them. In every café, morgue, and boutique, the goblins stopped to share tales of a singer with the voice of an angel and the head of a rather large squash.

And from Stabby Eye to Fiery Fork, among all the murmurings about a living girl who had escaped the City of Ether and a living cat with little to no fur roaming the desert, a new rumor emerged.

Unbeknownst to him, Pumpkin was becoming a legend.

Chapter Twenty-one

A Message to Isabella

Commander Berzerko floated through the cat door of the Hocus Pocus lighthouse and followed it all the way to the depths. She burst into the Bogey's room, where the Bogey was poised over a handwritten invitation to the water demons.

All Dark Spirits Must *Attend!*
Big Announcement at Midnight!

The Bogey jerked, smearing the last exclamation point. He listened nervously to the commander. Through her enraged meowings, the Bogey understood that the goblins and zombies had come back empty-handed. They had let the girl and her friends get away.

"Meow, meow, meow!" Commander Berzerko spat. Though she had searched the edges of the Petrified Pass and the Nothing Platte, she hadn't been able to catch a scent anywhere. Where were they?! Where were they hiding? And where were they headed next?

She coughed a hair ball onto the Bogey's desk for emphasis.

She met his eyes so that he knew she meant business. Then she stalked out of the room.

A map lay spread on the table of the colony's strategy room.

"Now, how were you plannin' to get into South Place?" Bertha asked.

May glanced at Beatrice, then back at Bertha. "Um, I guess we were going to go through the Hocus Pocus lighthouse."

Several people in the room let out a groan, Bertha's groan causing those around her to sway. Everyone waggled their hands in front of their noses.

Bertha shook her head. "A dangerous route. Isn't that right, Harley?" The man she had spoken to only twitched in the corner, muttering something about dust in the wind. May and Beatrice looked at Bertha questioningly.

"That's all he's done since he got back," she explained, "and that was twenty years ago. He had some kind of trauma down there in the dungeons." Bertha shrugged and shook her head. "Been absolutely hopeless ever since."

May gulped. There was something else weighing on her, and she needed to bring it up now or never.

"There's a boy in South Place. Lucius. I want to—"

"Out of the question," Bertha said, making a decisive chopping gesture with her hand.

"But—"

"We have a mess of undead risking their lives for this, and, honey, if you haven't noticed, life is precious in the Afterlife. A lot of us have lost spirits we love to the Dark Spirits. But you gotta be strong. Think of the big picture. We gotta get into the city, park ourselves somewhere." She thought, her upper lip twitching. "Hocus Pocus Horror Huts, most likely. Then we gotta get you into South Place fast—and get out fast once we get you in." She looked up at Pumpkin, who had started wearing a handkerchief over his mouth and nose to ward off Bertha's breath. Pumpkin whistled and looked off into the distance.

After ruminating a bit, Bertha let out a raggedy sigh. "The lighthouse is plumb dangerous. But it's probably the only option we have. A small group of us'll take you in."

She stuck her thumb on the place on the map where the lighthouse appeared and smiled gamely, a few bits of garlic plunking out and sticking on her wet lips. "Well, shoot. Down we go."

That night Bertha, May and her friends, and a select group of undead worked and reworked their plans for entering Hocus Pocus and South Place. Afterward Beatrice insisted on poring over the many newspapers, books, and magazines in the library. She and May read anything they could find on the city and its residents, just in case Bea's mother might be among them. "You never know," Bea said. "Every town is an opportunity."

A bottle of glowing ink perched on top of her papers, Bea carefully used her feather pen to copy any notes that seemed like they might be helpful. May sat beside her, trying to read up too, but fading fast. She rested her chin on her crossed arms and tried to stay awake. Somber Kitty curled into her lap and occasionally looked at her curiously, wondering when they were going to bed. He didn't dare venture away. Everywhere he walked, some eager colony member wanted to squeeze him tight or scratch his chin or—worse—talk to him in the goofy, high-pitched voice that humans sometimes used with animals as if they were complete dummies.

"Here's the name Longfellow," May said, slamming her finger on a roster for a bingo event at the Phantom Nuns' Parish, which had been held to raise money for clothes for people who died while skinny-dipping .

Beatrice leaned forward breathlessly. May read on, whipping her finger along the page. "'Scorecards were handed out by Captain J. T. Morgan and Henry Wadsworth Longfellow. . . .'"

Bea sighed and went back to her stack of papers.

About an hour later she folded her hands on top of the stack and looked at May solemnly. "I can't anymore. I'm tired."

Her bottom lip trembled just slightly. Bea pulled her legs up under her skirt, wrapping her thin, pale arms around them.

"That's okay," May said. "We can get up early and read more before we leave."

Beatrice's eyelashes fluttered gently as she looked at May. "You were right, back in the pass. I can't keep going like this." She looked down at where her feet were hidden under her dress. "I'm so tired, my toenails hurt."

May laughed, but it was a wheezy, kind laugh.

"All these years, and I've hardly thought about anything else. Maybe . . . I just need to let it go."

"Oh, no, Bea." May reached out for her friend's cool hand.

"I don't mean I want to *forget* her." Beatrice gave May a quivering smile. "I just mean that . . . maybe some things need to be meant to be. Do you know what I mean?"

May nodded. It made perfect sense.

"But . . . ," Beatrice warbled, on the verge of tears, "do you think I can stop missing her, May? Do you think spirits can change after all?"

"Oh, Bea." May's own eyes filled with tears, and she wrapped her arms around Bea, then pulled back and smiled at her. "I don't think you need to change a thing."

Beatrice smiled softly, let out a long sigh, then unfolded herself from her chair and floated out the door.

May stared after her. She longed to float down the hall and into bed too. But she turned back to Bea's stack of papers. If Bea gave up, who would look for her mom?

May pinched her cheeks to wake herself up and dug back into the stack.

A long while later, as May drooped over *Hocus Pocus Focus* magazine, her heavy eyelids just about to collide with her lower lashes, she spotted a paragraph buried in the classified section:

TYPHOID MARY'S CHATEAU FOR
SENTIMENTAL SICKLIES
88 Magnolia Lane, Hocus Pocus, T.E.A.

One of several homes owned by Typhoid Mary across the Ever After, we have catered to sickly spirits since 1920. Unless you lost them to gangrene or some other mishap, you'll love putting your feet up at this home away from life. Convenient to haunting locations. Affordable afterliving. Pick up your skull-o-phone and call now! Or send a telep-a-gram to the address above to reserve an apartment!

At the very least, it was worth a try. . . .

She tucked the paper under her arm and snuck around to the telep-a-booth down the hall. The telep-a-booth looked a lot like the teleporter beside it. But while the teleporter was for transporting souls, the telep-a-booth had an envelope symbol engraved on its glass door to indicate it was just for mental mail. May slid the door open and stepped inside the telep-a-booth.

A light appeared overhead, and she looked up to see RECIPI-ENT? spelled out in bright white letters.

May swallowed, read the address in the ad again, closed her eyes, and concentrated. *To Whom It May Concern, Typhoid Mary's Chateau for Sentimental Sicklies, 88 Magnolia Lane, Hocus Pocus.*

She looked up again. A shining envelope appeared, with the address across the front.

MESSAGE? the booth asked next.

May squeezed her eyes shut and thought again: *We're looking for a specter by the name of Isabella Heathcliff Longfellow. Um . . .* She looked up to see that her thoughts were being recorded on a large white glowing sheet of paper. She reached out to touch it, curious, but her fingers passed right through it. She tried not to think about words like "underwear" and looked up again. The message, so far, read:

We're looking for a specter by the name of Isabella Heathcliff Longfellow. Stop. Um. Stop. Underwear. Stop.

"Darn," May muttered. She didn't know how to erase it, so she just closed her eyes and tried to go on.

If she is there, please have her contact May Bird and Beatrice

Longfellow at—she remembered something Bertha had mentioned earlier—*at the Horror Huts Hotel in Hocus Pocus.*

She looked up.

Um, the end.

Colorful lights surrounded her head as the paper folded itself and disappeared into the opening of the translucent envelope addressed to the chateau on one side and now labeled on the other with SWAK. *Sealed With A Kiss.* It rose out of the hole at the top of the booth and then zipped up the chute.

May watched in awe. But a worry crept at the edge of her mind, like a mosquito whispering to her that she had made some kind of mistake she didn't comprehend. She considered going back into the library to read some more, but she was afraid she couldn't keep her eyes open another minute. Wearily, she floated down the hall to bed.

A few minutes later Somber Kitty, curled up beside Pumpkin, was the only one who saw the petals on Beatrice's necklace open, just slightly.

Late that night a mummy happened to be sitting on the porch of Typhoid Mary's Chateau for Sentimental Sicklies, resting his feet and drinking a slurpy soda, when a telep-a-gram arrived. The mummy watched the telep-a-gram float gently overhead, then land on the welcome mat with a flutter. Nosy, as most mummies are—even though their noses have long since fallen off—he picked it up and opened it.

When he got to the words "May Bird," he nearly choked on his soda. By that time, despite the Bogey's efforts to the contrary, May's reputation had preceded her—if not to the halls of Bo Cleevil's fortress in the Northeast, at least throughout the halls of South Place.

Taking the telep-a-gram with him, the mummy ambled off toward the lighthouse at top speed, in search of the Bogey.

Chapter Twenty-two

Who's Afraid of Hocus Pocus?

The Colony of the Undead was in a frenzy. Maps were dragged out of hidden crevices while a group of people locked themselves up in the strategy room and started banging around inside.

Lawless Lexy, who seemed to be Bertha's right-hand woman, led everyone through a crash course of lock picking, Dark Spirit detection, how to put a ghoul in a headlock, and other handy tricks for the journey. The entire group of undead jogged laps every morning without exception. They ran through an obstacle course of booby traps that spanned the entire area of their underground hiding place every afternoon, and they invited May and her friends to train with them. Fabbio often took the lead on these circuits, turning it into a race that nobody else was trying to win. Every time he arrived back at the starting line first, he twirled his mustache casually and tried not to show how hard he had tried.

Somber Kitty insisted on joining in on the martial arts lessons, though several of the undead snickered.

"Kitty, why don't you go curl up somewhere and relax?" Bea asked more than once. But Kitty merely looked at her coolly and executed his four-legged moves, balancing as best he could.

Pumpkin, trying to be more like Somber Kitty, often joined in too.

They were all given several bundles of notes on Hocus Pocus and South Place to study, curled tightly inside rubber bands. Pumpkin, who'd never used a rubber band before, shot them at every target he could think of, including Fabbio, who frowned at him irritably.

Everywhere May went, someone patted her on the back or smiled at her widely or even bowed with respect. Bertha had told everyone that she was going on secret business, but everyone assumed the business was to save them all, as *The Book of the Dead* had predicted. When May heard whispers about this, she ducked her head in shame. She couldn't get up the courage to deny their beliefs. So she said nothing.

On the day of May's departure the undead piled in for warm hugs, and May accepted them gratefully.

"No time to get sentimental, people. C'mon," Bertha said. "Now, nobody draw attention to themselves. Stay spread out on the Stubway—we'll all have our shrouds on, but we don't want a whole gaggle of Live Ones making themselves conspicuous. I'll take May and her friends. We'll all meet up at the Horror Huts Hotel. Remember, should something go wrong, we take the sewers out of town."

She was waving the group into the teleporter booth. One after another, five select undead, adorned in death shrouds, stepped in, plunked a tele-token into the slot, and disappeared.

May's pulse raced. She looked at her friends, who were

putting on brave faces, except for Pumpkin, who was trembling from big head to toe.

Amelia pushed her flight goggles up to her head and took May's hand. "I'm so proud of you. We know you can do it." She gave May a wink.

May felt a lump rise in her throat. She tucked Kitty safely underneath her shroud and plunked her token in the slot.

Chapter Twenty-three

A Gambling Town, a Rambling Town

HOCUS POCUS TRANSIT AUTHORITY.

"Here we are. Everybody out."

They all clambered out of the teleporter booth and stood in a knot at the front of the depot. Bertha waved everyone forward as they drifted through the crumbling stone doorway.

They followed the stairs down to a platform where several other spirits were waiting, looking at their watches, rifling through their briefcases. And then there was a sick, lopsided rumble from the dark tunnel to the right, and slowly, slowly, the Stubway emerged along the tracks.

It was a hulking, crooked thing, its windows cracked and its metal body rusted and full of holes. It lurched toward the waiting passengers forlornly, like an old dog.

The Stubway didn't so much come to a halt in front of them as simply expire in an exhausted sort of way. Pumpkin clutched the back of May's papoose, causing Somber Kitty, nestled inside, to let out a quiet groan. The travelers were jostled to and fro as they drifted into the train and spread out along the aisles.

"Pardon me. Excuse me. So sorry," Bea said.

Finally, they all settled in, and the doors creaked closed.

A voice came over a crackling loudspeaker above the handles. "Next stop, Wormhole."

At Wormhole a tall specter boarded and squeezed up next to May. He had clearly died in a fire, as tiny flames ran up and down his clothes. May couldn't help but stare at him out of the corner of her eye.

"Mind if I smoke?" he asked.

May was about to answer politely when the train made a hard turn to the right. All of the passengers were flung against the left wall. May fell into Bertha.

"Don't worry. Just the wormhole."

The train spiraled around and around, and then it emerged into the light of dusk, and they were back outside, moving slowly across the sand.

"What's that?" Beatrice asked, pointing out the window to a large, glowing blob in the distance, underneath a darkened sky.

"Hocus Pocus."

Bea took hold of May's hand, her delicate fingers digging in. Otherwise, she was the picture of calm. As they all stared out the windows intently, the city and its citizens began to take shape ahead of them.

Hocus Pocus was completely dead. That is to say, it was as lively a city as one could imagine in the Ever After. Spirits crowded the streets, ghosts promenaded across dilapidated overpasses. They crisscrossed, drifted, disappeared into this and that gambling hall or glowing green club with peppy organ music blaring out through its windows. Occasional fights tumbled out of the double doors of saloons onto the streets as hearses and horseless carriages jostled by. One spirit was jostled onto the tracks and yelled "Ouch!" as the Stubway ran over him.

A glowing sign hung over the tracks, burning brightly and sending lights disappearing into the dark, swirling stardust clouds above: A GAMBLING TOWN, A RAMBLING TOWN . . . WELCOME TO HOCUS POCUS.

Beyond the crooked, jam-packed roofs loomed the light-house. It was a dark black spire, fearsome to behold—every inch of it adorned with stone faces with gaping, fang-filled mouths. At its tip an enormous black light spun in circles, sweeping the sky with its heavy black shadow.

A ghoul crossing the street bumped into their train, grunted, and then rushed to catch up with a gang of ghouls up ahead. May bowed her head, tightening the hood of her shroud.

"Hey, Mister, room for one more?" one gaunt, dark-suited spirit asked, trying to drift into one of the windows. The car attendant threw him out. "Go buy a ticket, you deadbeat!"

The Stubway moved even slower now, on account of all the cars that pulled across the tracks ahead of it. Bertha muttered under her breath, something about Hocus Pocus drivers. May, Beatrice, Fabbio, and Somber Kitty had their faces pinned against the glass, mesmerized.

More glowing signs hung off the buildings at crooked, decrepit angles, advertising various attractions:

GHOULS, GHOULS, GHOULS! LIVE!

POLTERGEISTS ON ICE! ONE NIGHT ONLY!

SEE THE DREADED SILKIES MAGIC SHOW! YOU'LL BE AMAZED! ASTOUNDED! POSSIBLY ASPHYXIATED!

"May . . ." Beatrice waved to catch May's attention, then

motioned to the window in front of her, where May's breath had collected in a fog on the glass. Bea gestured that she should rub it off.

"Oh." May furiously shined it off with her fist. "Ahhh!" She fell backward. A gaunt lady in a long dress was looking at her through the glass and made a slicing motion across her throat.

Bertha grabbed her up tight, looking around nervously. "Silkies," she whispered. "Just cool your muffins." She casually waved her dagger at the woman, who only smiled wickedly and drifted away.

The Stubway took a hard left turn onto a new street off the main drag, slightly less crowded, and May and Bea gasped. On their right stretched the oily black waters of the Dead Sea. Several Dark Spirits were down on the beach, star bathing and socializing. Some pushed vending carts from one beach blanket to the next, peddling Putrid Pops and slurpy sodas.

On a rise to the left, a black-clad witch peered out of a window painted with FORTUNES, EARTH-COMPATIBLE HEXES, JUST IN TIME FOR HALLOWEEN.

"Oh, ohhhhh, can we please get a hex? What is a hex? What about a Putrid Pop?" Pumpkin was practically bouncing up and down.

"Here we are," Bertha said, turning a sharp-eyed look at Pumpkin, causing him to immediately shut his mouth tight. The train wheezed to a stop at the East Hocus Pocus Station.

The travelers drifted out of the car. They gathered for a moment on the platform and looked at one another. Bertha drifted under a billboard that read IF YOU DWELLED AT COFFIN VIEW

CONDOS, YOU'D BE HOME BY NOW! "No tail draggin' now, hear? Let's get a move on."

And with that, they followed her down an alley to a building shaped like a skull with a gaping mouth.

As soon as they'd secured rooms at the hotel, May went to the front desk to inquire after the telep-a-gram she'd hoped to receive from Typhoid Mary's, but there was nothing. Another dead end, she guessed. Upstairs, she watched Beatrice sadly. Bea was floating about the room, opening the curtains to let in the starlight and arranging the furniture to be a bit more homey. If possible, she seemed more melancholy than ever, though she wore a brave face.

If everything went as May hoped tomorrow, she wouldn't be around to see if Bea found her mother or not.

"Hey, Bea, do you want to take a walk with me?" May asked. Maybe they could share a slurpy soda. Or take in a poltergeist show.

Beatrice's eyes lit up. "Do you think we could?"

They both looked at Bertha, who was already busy sharpening a silver-tipped spear.

"I wish you wouldn't," Bertha said, seeming flustered. "It's a rough town." She eyed the girls' looks of excitement, seeming to give just a bit. "Well . . ." She leaned on one hip and gazed around the room. "Ohhh, I was a tadpole once. And as long as it's just you two. You can't take the cat, of course." Somber Kitty let out a discouraged meow from where he had curled up on the bed.

Bertha cast a look at Fabbio, who was staring at the parking lot and jotting down a haiku, then at Pumpkin, who had resurrected the handkerchief and put it back over his nose. "And I'm worried about those two." Bertha shook her head. "Just don't talk to strangers. And hurry back, ya hear?"

"Okay," May said, nodding. She pulled Bea out into the hallway.

"Strange things afoot today, girls," the innkeeper said from behind his desk as they drifted through the foyer. "Be careful out there. The Dark Spirits are restless."

They wound their way through the city streets, passing several large groups of ghouls and one smattering of goblins. Each time, they went stiff and quiet but tried their best to act naturally. And neither the goblins nor the ghouls seemed to take much notice of them.

Without having planned it, May found herself looking down each new street for Typhoid Mary's. She considered mentioning it to Bea but thought better of it.

And then there it was. Magnolia Lane.

May casually steered Beatrice to the right, the two girls drifting down the quiet, cobblestoned street.

About halfway down to the left, they came to it. The sign outside said TYPHOID MARY'S CHATEAU FOR SENTIMENTAL SICKLIES: SERVING THE TYPHOID COMMUNITY SINCE 1920. The building itself lay behind a stone archway, with a broad stone porch.

Beatrice took May's hand. "May, look," Beatrice said.

They drifted up the stairs onto the porch. A welcome mat at their feet announced FLOAT ON IN.

"Do you think we should go in?" Bea asked.

"We might as well," May said innocently.

Voices drifted down the corridor from a room at the far end of a long marble hallway just inside the front door. "Oh, maybe I'll just wait outside," Bea said. "I can't take another disappointment. Maybe you should go without me. And you can just . . . let me know."

"C'mon, Bea."

May held her friend's hand tighter as they drifted down the hall and up to the threshold.

The room was full of spirits in all types of old-fashioned clothes, from rags to beaded cocktail dresses with bits of lace at the throat. On a table was a big coffin-shaped cake with yellow writing: THEIR LOSS, OUR GAIN! HAPPY DEATH DAY, DOROTHY!

A woman, presumably Dorothy, was just blowing out her candles. Several of those spirits around her shook her hand and wished her well.

After a few more minutes May squeaked out an "Excuse me?"

Dorothy drifted their way. She wore a long, lavender dress, and her corn-colored hair was done up in a loose, old-fashioned bun. "Hello there. May we help you?" She looked back and forth between them with her sunken-in eyes.

"Yes." May cleared her throat. "We're looking for Mrs. . . . Mrs. . . . ." May looked at Beatrice to finish for her.

"Mrs. Isabella Heathcliff Longfellow," Beatrice practically whispered, then looked back at May.

"And we were hoping," May continued, "that you might know her."

Dorothy nodded. "I do."

May felt a shudder run through Bea's hand. She herself felt as if she'd just gone over the dip of a roller coaster.

"But she isn't here," Dorothy said, her hand playing with the lace collar at her throat. "What a shame. She left just this morning. For the City of Ether."

"But—but," May sputtered. "We sent a telep-a-gram!"

Bea shot her a wide-eyed look of surprise.

"I'm sorry," Dorothy said, sounding slightly offended. "We didn't receive any telep-a-gram. She goes away all the time." Dorothy sniffed, then added with gravity, "She'll be gone about a month or so. Looking for her daughter."

"But this *is* her daughter!" May shouted, waving Bea's hand at them.

Dorothy's dark eyes blinked, incredulous. "Oh?" she gurgled. "Oh, my! Oh, my dear! Truly?" She wrenched Bea's hand from May's and clutched it tighter, staring at her intently. "Why, yes! Yes, you are! You look just like her!"

Bea let herself be yanked all around like a rag doll. Her eyes had gone glassy.

"She talks about you all the time! She's been looking for you for *ages*! Oh, I'll dash off a telep-a-gram to her right away! She's riding the Bony Express! I know exactly which carriage. . . ."

Several spirits had congregated in the room now, hearing that Isabella's daughter had arrived. Many were wiping away tears while others were exclaiming how remarkable it all was. Still others murmured to Beatrice that her mother was a wonderful lady. But Bea appeared to be in shock. She just stood there.

"You come back here bright and early in the morning and see if we haven't heard back from her. Oh, my dear!" In her frenzy, several strands of corn-hued hair had worked themselves loose from Dorothy's bun and swung around her face, causing her to swat them away.

May looked at Beatrice for a response. But—nothing.

"Well, thank you," May said tightly, backing away, her heart pounding. "We'll be back in the morning."

"First thing tomorrow!" Dorothy practically shouted.

May floated Beatrice back down the corridor and outside onto the front steps, where she sat her down. "Bea?" She remembered something she had seen on TV about needing to pat people on the cheeks when they were unconscious. She tried this with Bea.

It failed to work for several minutes, but eventually, whether it was because of the patting or not, Bea finally turned to looked at May, her eyelids fluttering wildly like the tiny legs of a centipede bristling. Her eyes traveled over May's face in wonder.

"Tomorrow," she said. And then she fainted dead away.

That night May and Pumpkin sat awake by the window, watching as the inhabitants of Hocus Pocus drifted off to their graves for haunting time.

"May?" Pumpkin asked.

May looked at him. He seemed to have been thinking of something for a long time.

"I don't know if they'll let me come back anymore. To haunt your house. Now that I've skipped out on haunting duties for so long."

Pumpkin stared out the window, pensive. "Things in South Place will be dangerous," he finally continued. "If you make it home tomorrow, maybe we won't have a chance to say good-bye." Pumpkin's bottom lip trembled. He smoothed his tuft of hair nervously. "I just wanted you to know I've had . . . the best time ever."

May felt too sad to speak, but she managed to choke out: "And the worst."

They looked at each other and laughed.

"Having you as a friend makes me glad I was never born," Pumpkin joked, and they laughed again.

And then a tear dribbled from Pumpkin's eye, and May caught it with her finger.

"You won't forget me, will you?" he murmured, sucking in his bottom lip.

"Oh, Pumpkin." May wrapped her arms around him and hugged him tight. She pulled back and looked into his eyes. How could there be a life without Pumpkin? Even all the times, growing up, she hadn't known he was there, she now realized she'd felt him near her, and it had made her feel safe. "How could I forget my first friend?"

He was the first friend life had handed her—but also the first friend she had ever made herself. He had saved her from the water demon. Tackled the Bogey. Bargained with poltergeists. Sung goblins to sleep. . . .

With a start, May realized something else. "And you're *my* hero," she blurted out.

Pumpkin stiffened. He blushed. He looked back over his shoulder, then at May. "Does that mean you love me a little bit more than . . ." Pumpkin nodded his head toward Kitty, who lay on the bed watching them drowsily.

May stared at him, not sure what to say.

He waved his hands in the air and shook his head. "Don't answer that. You love us the same, right?"

"The same. And different," May replied finally, and strung her warm fingers through Pumpkin's cold ones.

A ghoul passed by outside the window, his slimy arms twitching. He filled both May and Pumpkin with the dread they had almost forgotten for a few minutes.

"It's getting so dangerous here in the Ever After," Pumpkin said, watching the ghoul until he slimed around a corner. He squeezed May's hand tighter. They sat for a long time in silence, and then Pumpkin said something that made May wince.

"I hope you never come back."

Chapter Twenty-four

A Long-lost Mother

Many light-years away Ellen Bird stood on the edge of a great tangle of plants. In her hand she carried a flashlight. In her pocket was a brown bag packed with sandwiches and nuts. On her feet she wore thick rubber boots over blue jeans.

As Ellen Bird set foot in the first prickly bush, she was almost sure she sensed the dimmest light flicker, somewhere deep and far ahead.

She was almost sure. But Ellen Bird had never believed in things she couldn't see.

She tromped into the briars.

Crash!

May was dreaming about her mother's brown curls when the silence of room 206 was shattered. Everyone tumbled out of their beds, staring at one another in a daze. Pumpkin smoothed his tuft. Fabbio jumped to attention.

Crash!

Except for Pumpkin, who zipped under the bed, the inhabitants of room 206 darted to the window, yanking open the curtains and peering outside.

Down on the street the city was in an uproar. Ghouls were chasing spirits with nets, goblins were rattling chains as they zipped after this specter and that ghost, slapping shackles around their legs and wrists and dragging them away.

"What's happening?" Beatrice asked.

They all turned to Bertha, who had already hurried to the door, her silver dagger in her hand, to peer through the eye-hole. She took a good look at the hall, then zipped back to the window.

"This is bad."

Outside, specters zipped out through the front door of the motel toward their carriages, trying to escape. Some were captured by zombies. Others managed to steer their carriages onto the street, only to be stopped just outside the parking lot.

Everville—or what had once been Everville—leaped into May's mind. "Are the Dark Spirits taking over?" she asked.

Bertha nodded once, heavily, as if she couldn't get up the energy to nod twice. Her mouth twitched, and her gray eyes took in the scene as sharply as an eagle. When they landed on some unknown sight, she gasped and shut the curtains tight.

"It couldn't be."

She peeked again and turned. "It is."

Bertha's eyes took on a fiery, fearful glint. She faced the others. "It's Commander Berzerko."

"Commander who?" May asked.

For the first time, Bertha appeared to be at a loss. She peered about the room wildly.

"Everyone, under the beds!" she snapped. The occupants

instantly did what they were told, grabbing their belongings and shimmying up against Pumpkin.

"If we open the door," Lawless Lexy whispered, "they'll think we've fled. So, everyone, be still!" She opened the door to their room, then quickly darted under the bed with the others. "As long as Berzerko doesn't sniff us out, we'll be okay."

Everyone cast glances at Bertha, but she didn't seem to notice. They waited with bated breath—some more bated than others—as they listened to the sound of ghouls pouring into the building.

Flip, flip, flip.

"Pumpkin, what is it you are doing?" Fabbio asked.

Pumpkin was flipping through Bea's Ghoulish-to-English dictionary. "I want to know if they're saying they're going to eat us!"

Everyone went still and listened.

"Gbbblebelbelebleeb! Gurrgllelelejjijj!"

"Let's hope they have souvenir stationery," Pumpkin translated in a whisper.

"Shhh!" everyone hissed back.

"Grlllllly bllllrrrrrrggggle!"

"And ice machines," he translated again, sticking his finger in his mouth fretfully.

"Shhh!"

The ghouls could be heard getting closer down the hall, followed by the sound of doors being opened. Then the door of their room creaked, and two pairs of slimy ghoul feet appeared in front of the bed, hurrying away just as quickly.

"Meow," Somber Kitty whispered, and May put her hand over his mouth.

"Meow." This time the meow had come from somewhere outside.

Somber Kitty and May looked at each other in the dark.

It was hours before the city of Hocus Pocus was quiet. The gang under the bed waited another hour after the ghouls had left before crawling out to peep, very carefully, through the blinds. They took in the scene below with dawning despair.

The city had been ransacked. Ghouls and goblins ambled through the streets, alongside groups of spirits in chains. More spirits were being added by the minute—caught in doorways and alleyways.

Below, a ghoul staked a sign into the ground from an armful of signs he was carrying:

PARDON OUR DUST! COMING SOON: CLEEVILVILLE #147.
COMING ATTRACTIONS: CRAWL-MART, CHAR-BUCKS, SKULLBUSTER VIDEO.
BROUGHT TO YOU BY YOUR FRIENDLY RULER, BO CLEEVIL.
REMEMBER, HE IS WATCHING YOU AT ALL TIMES.

"My mother," Beatrice said. "What if she comes back?" Fabbio scooted next to her and patted her head stiffly.

"No can do." Bertha turned to one of the chests of drawers and began retrieving her things, stowed inside. "We've got to head back to the colony." She looked at May solemnly. "There's no way you can get into South Place now."

"But—"

"No buts. We'll leave now. We'll use the sewers. It's confusing down there, but I know the way."

As Bertha packed, May noticed the watch she wore on her wrist. Under the glass face was a tiny skeleton. The skeleton had one long arm and one stumpy arm that was missing a hand. The stumpy arm pointed to the number 7, the long arm pointed to the number 2. It was 7:02 in the morning. May thought of Typhoid Mary's. They were supposed to be on their way there right now.

Bertha stopped her packing for a moment and turned to look at them. "Did anyone know you were coming here?"

May shook her head.

Bertha shook her head in response, bewildered. "It's as if they knew you were."

May's belly suddenly let out a painful *glurb*. Her telep-a-gram. Her face and ears felt like they had caught fire.

"My mother . . . ," Beatrice interjected.

"We can't wait for you," Bertha barked. "Too dangerous. And you'll never find your way out of the city on your own."

Beatrice trembled. She looked as if she might fall apart—cascade down onto the ground like a waterfall or cease to exist altogether. "But what if she comes back and . . . they catch her?"

Bertha cast her a pained, conflicted look. She peered at her watch, then out through the window and onto the street. She looked at May, who had already risen and was standing in the doorway, determined.

Bertha let out a husky groan. "If you two go, you go on your own. We can't go with you."

Beatrice nodded and floated to the doorway, reaching out to clutch May's elbow.

"You got an hour. I'll gather the rest of my crew in the

other hotel rooms and we'll take to the sewers at eight—not a minute after." Bertha adjusted her own shroud, then unhooked her watch and held it out toward May. "Here, take this. Be sure you get back. Trust me, this is not a place you want to be stranded without someone who knows the way out."

Minutes later May and Beatrice burst through the doors of Typhoid Mary's, looking about the hall wildly. It had been a death-defying trip through the streets of Hocus Pocus. Bea had almost walked right into a zombie, but May had pulled her back, and they'd ducked into a series of alleys, losing the zombie near an arcade. Then a troop of ghouls had filled both sides of their path, and they'd had to duck under a sewer grate.

Now Beatrice tugged at her dress as they hurried down the hallway. The watch Bertha had given May read 7:22.

"Let's split up. I'll meet you back here," May said, zipping off to one side of the building while Bea zipped off to the other. When they met again, the watch said 7:28.

"It's empty," May said, stricken.

"I know." Bea's lips were quivering. She looked completely dejected. There was no Dorothy, no telep-a-gram from Isabella, no anything.

They drifted back out to the front stairs. From here, they had a view down Magnolia Lane. Beyond it, the city gave way to a dusty road that led into a wide prairie, strewn with trash heaps and the occasional spooky shanty.

Seeing Bea's stricken face caused an earthquake in May's heart. She looked at the watch again. "We can wait here a little while, to see if a telep-a-gram comes," she offered.

Bea nodded numbly and sat. They stared off into the prairie. Every once in a while a cloud of vapor rising from one of the trash heaps drifted across the landscape.

When the skeleton watch pointed to 7:46, May began to fidget.

"How much time?" Beatrice whispered.

"Fourteen minutes." If they went at their absolute fastest and didn't run into any problems, May imagined it would take them at least eight minutes to get back to the Horror Huts.

"It'll come," Beatrice said, her eyes trained on the horizon. "She'll write and tell me where to meet her."

"I know you're right," May said. But she wasn't sure. In fact, she was beginning to believe the opposite was true.

"I know it doesn't make sense," Bea said, her voice creaky. "But I just feel it. I *feel* we need to stay here."

A minute passed. As May began to tug Bea upward, her eyes traveled to Bea's neck. "Bea, look!"

The flowers on Bea's necklace were in full bloom.

They stared at it a moment. "What do you think it means?" Bea whispered.

May tugged her hand. "I don't know. But we have to go."

And then a movement on the prairie caught their eye, and they turned to look.

It resembled a cloud of vapor, but this one seemed to be moving purposely toward them. It disappeared behind a pile of trash for an instant, then reappeared around the nearer side.

Bea stood stock-still. She didn't seem to be able to move.

The figure became more defined by the second. It sorted itself into a shape before their eyes.

"That's her suitcase," Bea said. "That's her dress."

May squinted, but she could hardly make out a thing. Still, the figure seemed to spot them, because it came to a full stop. And then a sound drew the figure's attention to the left. A troop of ghouls had wandered into the prairie on the west end. They, too, had spotted the lady with the suitcase and were starting to make their way toward her, first floating slowly, unsure, and then picking up speed.

Bea followed the woman's gaze.

"Gblbblblbelbelebeleb!"

Time seemed to freeze. And then Bea found her voice. "Mama, *run!*"

The ghouls began to zip now, but Bea's mother didn't run. She started to sway. "May, do something!"

May didn't think. She only acted. She grabbed her bow from her back and zipped forward.

Chapter Twenty-five

Going Down

Without a word, the lady dropped her suitcase and backed away, tripping over the hem of her dress.

Reaching her a moment before the ghouls, May pulled an arrow taut along her bow and aimed at the foremost ghoul. Her arm shook, but the line of ghouls skidded to a halt, colliding into each other and jabbering.

Bea caught up just behind May. "Mama!" she cried, throwing her arms around the woman.

May stole a glance over her shoulder, almost unable to believe her eyes. Her fingers trembled on the string.

"Beatrice!" Isabella whispered.

The ghouls started to drift forward. Biting her lip hard, May let an arrow fly. This time it zipped into the air, covering about half the distance to her target, and then froze . . . and fell. The ghouls watched it with their mouths open. When it was clear the arrow would not magically rise again from the ground, they let out loud howls of laughter.

May looked back at mother and daughter, hanging on to each other for dear life. She slung her bow over her back, backing up. "Let's go!"

With the ghouls clambering after them, they zipped like lightning into the streets of Hocus Pocus, not bothering to duck and hide when a Dark Spirit crossed their path. Most spirits were so shocked to see them moving so boldly that they stopped and stared before they gave chase. Others tried to grab them, swiping at them. One managed to get hold of Beatrice's sash, and it came off in ribbons.

Spirits closed in on all sides of them until a horde was on their tail down the main boulevard.

"We've got to lose them," May shouted over her shoulder, and zipped into a side street, then another and another, counting on Bea and Isabella to keep up. When she looked over her shoulder and saw that they were, at least temporarily, alone, she veered in the direction of the Horror Huts, praying she'd be able to find the group. And suddenly, there they were, at the gaping, smiling skull face that marked the back entrance. Bertha and the others—Fabbio, Pumpkin, and Somber Kitty included— were just coming down the hall. Bertha looked angry, relieved, and intent all at once. Somber Kitty leaped at May, dangling on her shroud before she swooped him into her arms. He gave her an earful of reproachful meows.

"Righty," Bertha said. "Let's go."

The sewer that led out of the city had an opening four blocks away, and the group made their way quickly, Beatrice and Isabella clinging to each other all the while, as if one or the other might vanish at any moment. May followed just behind Bertha, occasionally looking behind her and casting a triumphant glance at the two. They weren't out of trouble yet, but close.

As they ducked down alleys, they could hear loud groups of spirits combing the streets, roaring and snarling, in an uproar again over the three specters who'd streaked the boulevard so boldly.

"What'd you guys do?" Bertha growled. "Ring the dinner bell?" Then she thrust a finger forward, indicating an alley across the way and a tiny metal sewer grate protruding from the road. But May's attention had been drawn to something else poking above the building at the end of the alley.

Once the coast was clear, the group darted across the street, May following along blindly, her eyes pinned to the thing above the rooftops.

"Everybody in," Bertha said, grunting with the weight of the sewer grate as she lifted it and ushering her people—and then Pumpkin, Fabbio, Bea, and Isabella—down into the sewer. But May had drifted past them, farther down the alley, to its very edge.

Here, the tight alleys of the city opened up to the beach. And there, in the middle of the sand, perched on the very edge of the sea and mounted on a pile of black rocks, was the lighthouse.

Above the doorway was an ornate, carved stone banner, which could only be read when the light shone through it. What it said sent chills down into May's heart: ABANDON HOPE ALL YE WHO ENTER HERE.

"May! Let's go!"

May swiveled. Bertha was standing halfway out of the sewer, waving her on with her dagger. Pumpkin had poked his head out too and was staring at May, nibbling on a finger. He looked at her hopefully.

May looked down at Kitty snuggled tightly in her arms. She looked at Bertha, whose mouth suddenly settled into a sad, grim line, as if she understood. And then she looked at Pumpkin, her heart pounding painfully. She thought of her mother. She thought of how much safer her friends would be without trying to help her. And then she set her jaw.

May turned and floated away.

"May!" Pumpkin howled behind her, so loudly that his voice sounded hoarse. But May didn't look back. Not until the sound of his cries became muted and echoey.

When she did turn, Bertha and the others were gone, and the sewer grate was back where it belonged.

May swallowed. She hugged Kitty tight. And then she turned forward again, checked the beach, and zipped toward the lighthouse.

Part Three

Under the Sea

Chapter Twenty-six

The Dark Spirit Capital of the Universe

Commander Berzerko roamed the empty streets of Hocus Pocus, her ear tilted to the slightest sound, her nose pointed to the cobblestones, sniffing. The cat and his girl had been here, she was sure of it. And so it boggled her mind that she couldn't catch their scent.

Ghouls and goblins ran the streets with the last of their prisoners. Commander Berzerko watched them indifferently, cleaning her paws, staring up at the nearby buildings darkly. Where were they? It was almost time for the festivities to start, which meant her time above was up.

Hearing a sound, she turned but saw nothing. Only the lighthouse standing behind her, surrounded by empty beach.

She sniffed the air one last time.

Then she let out a reluctant meow and jumped into the waters of the Dead Sea, returning to the realm below.

Glurb, glurb, glurb.

As May descended the spiral stairs, pushing ever farther downward, her death shroud cast a faint glow around her as if she were a lightning bug falling from the sky. Around her, the sea gurgled and glubbed and bubbled. It seemed to call to her, enticing her down, down, down.

Pausing to look upward, May searched for a speck of light coming from above, but there was nothing. She gazed downward again, unsurely, and then continued.

After nearly an hour of descending, May began to wonder if she had somehow taken the wrong stairs or come through the wrong lighthouse, although the ABANDON HOPE sign seemed to be a pretty good indication that this was the place. The stairs seemed to plummet endlessly onward, so that even Kitty squirmed impatiently where May had tucked him under her shroud.

Under her breath, May hummed "My Favorite Things." But that made her think of Pumpkin and his shocked expression when she left, so she stopped.

She began counting stairs and had already counted to 2,007 when she slammed into a wall. May stuck her hands out in front of her and felt around. Besides the stairs that led up, she was surrounded by only walls.

Panic rose up inside her. May pulled Somber Kitty out of her shroud and set him down, then felt blindly along the walls with her hands, looking for a latch, a knob, something, squinting in the dim light.

Sniff. Sniff.

She crouched and felt for Kitty. He had his nose pressed up against one of the walls, smelling it, and May let her fingers travel along his snout to the place where he was sniffing. There was a tiny, uneven hole.

May rubbed her finger against it, perplexed.

"Meay," Kitty whispered, equally perplexed.

May sank onto the stair behind her and crossed her arms. And then she remembered. The key!

She dug into her left, then her right pocket and grasped the small, cool piece of metal. She pulled it out, feeling for the hole again. "Cross your paws, Kitty," she whispered. She stuck it into the hole. A perfect fit.

She gave it a small twist, and the floor disappeared from underneath her.

May landed with a splash flat on her back, then came up spluttering. "Uck," she grunted, wiping the smelly slime off her face. She was in a trough of some sort, feeding a waterwheel at one end of a stream.

She had only a moment to feel extremely proud of having made it this far before she noticed a pair of slitted eyes glowing at her in the dark. Kitty perched expertly on the edge of the trough, completely dry and flapping his tail casually.

May was about to stick out her tongue at him teasingly when a movement caught her eye, and she ducked back into the muck, pulling Kitty with her. She leaned forward on her elbows.

A few specters stood at the far end of the trough, gathering up slime in buckets. And then a ghoul appeared from around the waterwheel, gabbling at them.

"Hbblblgbglblg!"

The ghouls urged the specters onward, in the opposite direction. Prisoners, May assumed, though none of them wore shackles. Every one of them had stooped shoulders, their eyes cast to the ground.

When the group had passed, May and Kitty sat up again and slowly, slowly, climbed out of the trough.

A cobblestoned street stretched before them, lit with a dim purple light and lined on one side by a wide, dismal field. Floating in the air, just at the field's nearest edge, were glowing purple letters that read: MAP.

Just as she started toward it, a noise drew May's attention upward, and she shrank back into the shadows. Overhead, black gondolas slid greasily along, suspended by nothing. Most of them were empty, but there was the occasional cartful of goblins or ghouls jabbering along. Beyond them, there seemed to be no sky and no ceiling, either—only a gray haze drifting far above.

May waited for a break in the gondola traffic, then she and Kitty zipped across the street to look at the map. It was a three-dimensional spiral, showing a river moving down, down, down through the middle of the place, like a corkscrew. Tiny stars floated on the river's surface, marking areas labeled CORKSCREW RIVER, DEAD SEA MILL, PHLOAT-IN PHANTASMAGORIA, GHOUL VILLAGE, GOBLINS GROTTO, SWAMP OF SWALLOWED SOULS, WILD HUNT MANOR, ZOMBIE PITS, RECEPTION HALL.

"The Corkscrew River," May whispered, pointing to the spiraling, flowing line she had noticed first. "That's our way. It looks like we just need to follow it to the bottom."

As her pinky touched the map, a tiny, ghoulish face appeared. *You Are Here.* It looked like the river was just across the field.

May scooped Kitty under her arm and darted in that direction, casting a look at the gondolas above, which were still empty. In a few moments they arrived at the mouth of the river.

A gangplank led to an area where several empty rafts had been corralled. A sign stood beside the gangplank.

WELCOME TO SOUTH PLACE: DARK SPIRIT CAPITAL OF THE UNIVERSE

MAYBE YOU'VE ALWAYS BEEN EVIL. OR MAYBE YOU BECAME A BAD EGG LATE IN LIFE. IN ANY CASE, AT SOME POINT, YOU WENT ROTTEN TO THE CORE, AND THAT'S WHY YOU'VE BEEN DIRECTED TO OUR REALM, WHERE YOU'LL FIND YOURSELF AMONG LIKE-SPIRITED SPIRITS. HERE IN SOUTH PLACE, WE HAVE SO MUCH TO OFFER YOU. WE TORMENT THE LIVING AND SO MUCH MORE . . .
EVIL.
IT'S JUST MORE FUN.

May blinked at the sign a few times. Then she turned to spot a poster like the kind one might find at a travel agency hanging in the air nearby. It showed two zombies and a goblin enjoying a game of Scrabble with the headline IF YOU'RE LOOKING FOR YOUR WORST NIGHTMARES TO COME TRUE, YOU'VE COME TO THE RIGHT PLACE!

May and Somber Kitty looked at each other. "Meow," he said.

"I agree," May said, assuming he meant, *Let's get out of here.*

They climbed onto one of the empty rafts and pushed off.

Chapter Twenty-seven

A Luminous Boy

The Corkscrew River made a slow, greasy spiral downward.

Occasionally, the water lapped up the sides of the raft, making May and Kitty huddle in the middle of it and stare uneasily at its many holes and the dingy, frayed ropes that held it together.

When rafts full of Dark Spirits passed by, May and Kitty ducked. Some rafts held specters with daggers and thieves with masks like raccoon eyes and handkerchiefs tied around the lower parts of their faces. Some held creatures even more hideous than the ones May had seen already in the Ever After.

On either shore they could see the sights of South Place. To the right, atop a crooked hill, perched a village full of small, jagged stone houses, with windows like gaping eyes. A handful of prisoners clambered up and down the hill with buckets, fetching water from the river. Ghouls stood in the streets bartering, jabbering, drinking slurpy sodas, and pushing around their captives.

The raft drifted into oily black rapids and then crested a small waterfall. May crouched, pulling her shroud hood over her and Kitty to block him from the spray.

Several black skyscrapers sprung up on either side of the river, stabbing the misty, skyless sky. One misshapen monstrosity of a building straddled the river. Across its base, which arched over the water, were the words:

THE CHAMBER FOR DARK SPIRIT RELATIONS:
CONVINCING THE REALM WE AREN'T UP TO NO GOOD,
WHICH OF COURSE WE REALLY ARE

As the raft drifted under the building, a voice came over a hidden loudspeaker in the echoey, drippy dark:

"Dominating the Afterlife is only one of the many hats we wear here in the dark realm under the sea. Just like other spirits, we haunt Earth. Here are a few of the services we perform on our distant, living cousin planet:

- *"Horrific hauntings*
- *Taking advantage of kind old ladies*
- *Inspiring terrible nightmares*
- *Internet pop-ups*
- *General torment and misery."*

They floated out from under the building and over another waterfall.

Down, down, down they went. May felt the world above getting farther and farther away as they floated past dark villages, gaping caves with fearsome murmurings coming from inside, and decrepit bridges that snaked their way over the water, looking like they might collapse at any moment.

On the fifth floor down, May and Somber Kitty floated past a black, bubbly, howling swamp. A crooked sign announced it to be the CAVERN OF THE SWAMP OF SWALLOWED SOULS. Shortly after came an enormous manor, with black hedges pruned in the shapes of gargoyles, arched windows shrouded in darkness, turrets spiking up from the roofs, and pillars guarding the great front doors. In the foreground was a large hedge maze and a great lawn.

After that came a wide-open space full of Dark Spirits, all sitting in the shadow of a craggy mountain. High up, an arching, glowing purple sign read PHLOAT-IN PHANTASMAGORIA.

Beneath the sign, a giant ghoul, at least twenty feet high, moved back and forth to the oohs and aahs of the spectators who were watching. May let out a squeal and ducked just as one of the ghoul's arms moved above the raft, then swept back to land. She raised her eyes and peered over the side to see where it had gone, and then gasped.

It was only a projection.

As they floated on through, peering over the lip of the raft while lying on their bellies, May and Somber Kitty watched the giant holo-movie being projected into the air.

The film, which was silent and completely three-dimensional, showed two ghouls whistling and walking along the sea, looking pensive. Loud sniffles rose from the crowd. A song played in the background. It sounded a lot like "Wind Beneath My Wings," one of May's mom's favorite songs.

The raft rounded a corner. As it did, May's eyes fell back to the crowd, and she saw something that made her limbs go tingly.

He was with a group of other captives, handing out slurpy

sodas to greedy, grabby ghoul hands. He looked beaten and almost . . . *withered*, his soul wispy-looking and dimmer than it had been the last time she'd seen him. His back arched over his work, and his head hung down on his neck, not a hint of mischief or youth in his posture, not a touch of light.

He was no longer luminous. But he was Lucius, no mistake.

At first Ellen Bird thought she was imagining things.

Up ahead, through an opening in the briars, she saw something she had never seen in all her years living in dry, droughty Briery Swamp. A lake.

Slowly, carefully, she pushed the last of the briars aside with her feet. Her boots squelched as she stepped onto the soft muddy ground of the clearing and looked up at the dusky, cloudless sky.

Suddenly, with a sound like a giant light switch being flicked, the lake lit up.

Ellen, startled, took a step backward against the vines.

"Ouch!" She pulled forward again and gazed about. Nothing around her had changed, except the lake was glowing like a television set.

Wringing her hands together nervously, Ellen made her way slowly to the water's edge, until her toes came right up to it. She leaned forward and peered in.

Chapter Twenty-eight

The Rescue of Lucius

The raft drifted into a cave lined by spindly walking paths on each side. May gazed over its back end at the purple light of the opening they had just come through, smoothed her bangs to either side of her forehead, and looked at Kitty. And then she stuck her hands in the water and began to stroke furiously.

Kitty looked at her like she'd lost her mind.

As soon as she had gotten close enough to the wall of the cave, she reached out and tried to jam her hands into a crevice. The current was too strong, though. By the time May finally managed to slow the boat, they were nearing the other side of the cave. May swept Kitty into her right arm and leaped onto the small dirt path.

As she landed, she remembered she should have somehow anchored the raft, but when she turned, it was already drifting away quickly, carried by the current.

May swallowed. And then she and Kitty made their way back toward the light.

At the lip of the cave the two paused and peered up along the bank of the river. No view of Lucius. May scrambled up the rise, Kitty reluctantly following right at her heels. They both ducked behind a rock.

Up in the air ahead, the phantasmagoria flickered. As the Dark Spirits in the audience jabbered, shushed one another, and sucked on their slurpy sodas, May scanned the crowd again for Lucius and caught a glimpse of him, drifting over by the concession stand. May looked about for a way to get his attention.

Before she could think of one, the last scene of the movie flickered to an end, and the ghouls began to move around, stretching their arms and blowing their noses.

As a couple of ghouls gestured and jabbered loudly, the prisoners started moving, Lucius among them. And May and Somber Kitty followed.

The ghouls and their captives disappeared down a series of alleys, then into a cave. Slinking in the purple shadows, May and Kitty trailed them, looking like flies drifting into a yawning mouth.

Through curving tunnels, they drifted on, May and Kitty shrinking back into nooks and crevices when the ghouls turned to chatter at one another. Lucius did not turn around or even swivel his head to the side, and May began to doubt herself, wondering if it was really him. They got farther and farther away from the river, curving this way and that.

Soon the group ahead came to an opening, and everyone stopped.

The ghouls shouted at their captives, directing them forward.

May and Kitty waited until they'd all gone ahead, then crept into a niche to the left and, hidden, took in the incredible sight around them.

They had come to an enormous cavern lined on all sides with rocks, smelly black water dribbling down their jagged edges. The walls of the cavern rose so high that no ceiling was in sight—only a gray, filmy mist. Slimy dark algae clung to the rocks and hung down in soppy wet strings. And here and there, nestled into crannies in the rocks, were what looked to be a thousand or more goblins.

Some were sleeping, some were gathered in groups listening to music or watching holo-vision, some were doing their nails or modeling clothes for one another. They smiled at each other with their impossibly long fangs, then occasionally tried to push each other off the rocks. One succeeded from time to time, its victim dashing against the rocks below and then slowly climbing back up again, laughing and pretending to think it was a good joke. And then it would reach the perpetrator and try to gnaw off one of its limbs.

A gaggle of them was dangling from the ceiling doing circus tricks.

Trash was strewn everywhere: shopping bags, dirty socks, discarded clothing, old tiaras. The prisoners dispersed among the trash and began to pick it up, dropping it into heavy black sacks.

Her heart pounding, May kept her eyes on Lucius, whose back was still to her. He was picking up one of the old socks sluggishly, too defeated to be disgusted. He merely let go of the sock and swiveled toward the next piece of trash.

May looked at Somber Kitty, wondering what to do to get Lucius's attention. But Kitty saw what she wanted and acted quickly, backing his hindquarters up to the edge of the crevice that hid them and waving his tail at Lucius. Lucius turned his dull eyes toward the motion, curiosity crossing his face briefly. He looked at his captors, who had sat down to a game of pinochle.

May and Kitty sank back into the crevice and waited with bated breath. Presently, an arm appeared in the open space, picking up a pink feather boa that was lying on the ground. And then Lucius's face appeared, peering in at them surreptitiously. His eyes widened, and at the same time, a tiny hint of a glow lit him up from the inside.

There was no time to lose. May leaped forward and, stretching as far as she could, grabbed him by the collar of his blue jacket, slapped a hand over his mouth, and pulled him backward.

Lucius tried to let out a startled yell, but Somber Kitty leaped on his chest, with back arched, and the yell died in his throat.

Lucius lay there, flat on his back, his eyes moving to May's. For a moment a big, mischievous smile started creeping to his face, but then something else seemed to dawn on him, and his face went dark and stormy.

"What are you doing?" he hissed. He swept Kitty aside and stood up, glaring at May.

She held her finger to her lips. "Saving you. Shhh."

Lucius took this in, then shook his head furiously. "Uh-uh. No thanks. You've done enough already."

Somber Kitty, who'd run to the head of the crevice to keep watch, gave them both an annoyed look, and they both shut their mouths tight. Lucius backed up against the wall opposite May, looking alarmed and unsure whether to stay or flee.

May stared at the opening until, eventually, she felt Lucius eyeing her. Her cheeks burned.

"Something's different about you," he finally whispered.

"I'm deader than before," May murmured, annoyed. She had never told Lucius she actually wasn't dead at all—and she wasn't about to now.

Lucius considered this, then shrugged. "I don't really fancy being rescued by a girl, half dead or all dead. Especially one who got me trapped in an underworld of eternal torment and misery."

May rolled her eyes at him. He kept his profile to her. He had the same messy blond hair, blue eyes, and flushed cheeks that May remembered. He was still taller than her, still older than her. But the smile was missing.

May softened. What he'd said was true.

"Especially one as inept as you," he added.

May crossed her arms in front of her stomach. She didn't even know what the word "inept" meant. "I think *you're* the one who's inept."

Kitty looked back over his shoulder and again scolded them with his glare.

"Sorry," she whispered to Kitty.

They stood awhile, listening to the sounds of the goblins echoing around the cavern, nobody knowing quite what to do next.

"What are you doing with a cat, anyway?" Lucius finally asked.

Somber Kitty pulled his small death shroud closer with his teeth.

"Long story." May gave Lucius a hard look. "Now, do you want to escape or not?"

Lucius looked surprisingly indifferent as he thought about it. Finally, he shrugged. "All right. I'm in. We should stick something in their ears," he said. "I have all sorts of things I've nicked. Ecto-spasm syrup, Specter Spew shampoo, Soul Shrinker . . ."

"That'll never work," May said. She didn't know what those things were, but she knew it was crazy to try to confront all those goblins. They'd have to sneak out. It couldn't be that hard, since they'd snuck their way in. "How do we go down from here?" she asked.

Lucius stuck his chin in the air. "*Why* would we go down?"

May paused. "Um. I need to get something."

"From where?"

"The Bogey's bedroom."

Lucius's faint glow flickered. His pretty blue eyes turned wide and scared, and then his eyebrows descended darkly.

"You must be joking."

Somber Kitty eyed him to let him know they couldn't be more serious.

Lucius shook his head and began to back away. "No. Definitely not. I won't go."

"But . . ."

Lucius quickly drifted backward toward the mouth of the crevice. At the same moment Somber Kitty let out a hiss, and May swiveled to look behind her, a tiny yelp escaping.

She was faced by a creature directly in front of her, floating at shin height.

It was black and fluffy, with a pink bow in its hair. It stared at her and let out a tiny mew.

"Poor thing!" May whispered, reaching out toward it. Where were all these cats coming from? This one looked a lot like the one they'd seen at Risk Falls. Behind her, Somber Kitty growled.

"Mew?" the cat asked sweetly, tilting its fluffy head, its pink bow leaning jauntily to the right.

"Here, little kitty," May whispered. "I won't hurt you."

She expected the cat to either run away or float toward her shyly, but she did not expect what happened next. The small creature floated higher and higher into the air and began to puff out like a balloon.

In another second Somber Kitty had leaped between May and the black cat, his fuzz standing on edge, his tail straight as a flagpole, his teeth bared.

"Kitty? What—?" She reached for him, but as she did, something yanked her backward by the waist, and she let out a scream. Out of the corner of her eye she could see Lucius, squirming and struggling in the strong, stubby arms of a goblin.

"Kitty!" May's eyes shot to where Kitty had been floating just a moment before. But he—and the cat with the pink bow—were gone.

Ellen Bird stood on the lake's edge, mesmerized by something she saw inexplicably far beneath the surface. It appeared to be a point of light floating up toward her.

As it got closer, the light took the shape of a figure. And the figure got larger and larger, like it was coming from somewhere very deep, deep down. It looked to be a woman, now that it was closer. A beautiful woman with hair swirling all around her. The woman flipped and twisted as gracefully as a water dancer.

When the mysterious swimmer was only a few feet away, her eyes met Ellen's. She smiled, and all of Ellen's worries and fears and sadness of the past months seemed to melt away. The frown on Ellen's lips—that frown that had been there since the day May had gone—slipped off of her face. Ellen Bird sighed, feeling amazingly peaceful. The woman's smile seemed to say, I see you. I understand you. I know.

Chapter Twenty-nine

The Dungeons of Abandoned Hope

May looked about. She was in a colorless, square room, open on one side. Lucius lay in a ball in the corner, hiding his face. Kitty was nowhere to be seen.

Posters hung on one of the walls covered with phrases like: WHY TRY? and ALL WE ARE IS DUST IN THE WIND. A book sat on a tiny table nearby: *Life: A Whole Lotta Trouble For Nothin'*. May stood up on wobbly legs and walked toward the side of the room where there was no wall, but as soon as she reached the threshold, there was a loud *zap!*

"Ouch!" May grabbed her elbow and backed up.

"Invisible bars, silly."

May swiveled. Lucius had sat up and was gazing at her forlornly.

"I've got to get Somber Kitty," she said, turning back to the invisible bars. She reached out to push against them. Again, they zapped her hands. Undefeated, she kicked them. Then she tried to ram them, getting her shoulder and her back zapped over and over.

Finally, she stood back, clenching her fists. "No!" she yelled. "No! No! No!"

She felt Lucius's arm go around her and pull her away from the bars. They sat down next to each other. "My cat," she said, looking at him mournfully.

"These dungeons are impossible to break out of," Lucius said. "The prisoners whisper about it. They say the one wall's invisible just to tease you."

At that, without warning, May burst into tears.

Instead of scolding her or telling her she sounded like a baby or saying she had gotten them here in the first place, Lucius patted her knobby left knee awkwardly.

"I won't go home without him," May murmured.

"Where's home?"

May looked up at him. He was looking at her with the utmost earnestness.

"Home is where my mom is."

Lucius stared at her solemnly.

She swept back the cuff of her shroud and showed Lucius her arm—not translucent, not glowing. "I'm alive." She pulled back her death shroud to reveal how colorful she was, how solid.

Lucius took this in calmly, almost sadly.

"Aren't you surprised?"

He shrugged. "Disappointed."

"Why?"

"Well, being dead seemed to be the only thing we had in common." He grinned.

May didn't laugh. She just hung her head.

"Look on the bright side. At least the goblins thought you were dead."

"How do you know?"

"Well," Lucius folded his hands, "if they knew you were a Live One, we'd be getting a visit from the Bogey right about now."

They both looked down the corridor as if the Bogey were about to appear in front of them.

"Look." Lucius shifted. "You may be surprised by how things turn out. Take me, for example. Yesterday I thought being a slave to ghouls was the worst thing that could happen to me. Now I'm in a dungeon."

"I'm so sorry. For everything."

Lucius's eyes sparkled the way they had back in the Catacombs. "It was brave of you to try."

May rolled her eyes. "Yeah."

"Anyway, seeing you makes me feel more like my old self." Lucius shifted again and cleared his throat. May smiled, trying to be optimistic. She wondered where Fabbio, Beatrice, and Pumpkin were at that moment. Hopefully, far out of Hocus Pocus. At least they were safe. But still, being away from them made her feel very alone.

May and Lucius were quiet for a while.

"So, did you come all this way just to find me?" he eventually asked.

"Well . . ." May fidgeted. "I was *hoping* I would find you. But actually, like I said, I'm trying to get home. The Lady of North Farm told me there's a way, under the Bogey's bed."

Lucius tilted his head thoughtfully and turned to face her. "I thought that was just a tall tale."

"What?"

Lucius blinked. "Well, that the Bogey has his own personal

portal to Earth. Everybody whispers about it. Gosh, and to think it's been there all this time." Lucius's eyes brightened, along with his whole body. "I could go back to Earth with you." And then, just as quickly, his glow faded. He seemed to wilt like a flower. "It was 1942 when I died. I suppose I wouldn't have much to go back to now." And then another thought seemed to occur to him, and he went a shade or two even dimmer. "I suppose that's how the Bogey got me. By coming through that portal of his."

May felt anger bubble up. She remembered hearing how the Bogey had stolen life from Lucius and the other luminous boys, by entering their nightmares. She took the fabric of her death shroud in both hands and picked at it.

Lucius tugged on the tie of his private school uniform. "It's a shame really, about the bars. There's a great shortcut just down the hall there." He pointed. "The Lazy Way Ladder goes straight to the top, with an entrance on each level."

May followed his gesture skeptically. "How do you know?"

Lucius grinned, puffing out his chest. "I know this place backward and forward. Picking the Fruits of Bitterness here. Digging ditches there. I've had to carry ghoul laundry"—he wrinkled his nose—"through half the hallways and corridors down here. I don't need a girl to rescue me."

May tried to ignore how annoying he could be. "Well, if that's true, why haven't you escaped already?"

Lucius considered this seriously for a long moment. "Hope, I guess."

"Hope?"

"Well, when you don't hope for anything, I suppose you don't really bother, do you?"

"No." May shook her head. "I guess not."

"I mean"—Lucius leaned back and stared at the low, color-less ceiling—"it's silly, but I've sort of just stopped hoping to get out. Maybe it's the air here."

"Or a shadow," May said, thinking of the heavy darkness that seemed to fill everything Bo Cleevil and the Dark Spirits touched.

"And then, of course, there's the Bogey," Lucius added.

May leaned toward him sympathetically, not quite bold enough to touch his hand. She knew that he had been petrified of the Bogey ever since he had died.

They sat and stared at each other for a while.

Then, suddenly, Lucius slapped himself on the forehead. "I know how we can get out of here!"

May looked at him like he'd grown a third head. "Really?"

"Yeah, come on. Let's go."

May looked around. "How?"

"Well, we'll just asport."

"Asport?"

"*Asport,* silly. You know, disappear and reappear. It's not easy, but if you practice enough, any spirit can do it. It's like whistling or blowing a bubble."

May looked around. "But wouldn't the Dark Spirits know that? Wouldn't they make sure you couldn't asport out of here?"

Lucius thought about this. "Well, you can asport only a few feet. And most spirits don't know how."

May nibbled her pinky nail. "Well, I don't think I can asport anyway. I'm not a spirit."

Lucius wilted immediately. "Oh." He looked about. "Right . . .

I hadn't thought about that." For a few minutes his glow dimmed. And then he knelt in front of her and gave her his old devilish smile. "Just try it."

"Oh, I don't—" Just then the thought *Why try?* crossed her mind. May looked at the poster across the dungeon. And then she looked back to Lucius, who was staring at her earnestly.

"If you think about it," he continued, "being here in the lowest depths of South Place is the pits. But it is also something else."

"What?"

"It's the closest you can get to the Bogey's bedroom."

Through the empty hallways of South Place, Somber Kitty and Commander Berzerko careened like pinballs. When Somber Kitty zipped left, so did the commander. When he zipped right, the commander was right behind him.

The chase took them up the spiral of South Place, along the Corkscrew River. As Somber Kitty zipped past them, Dark Spirits of every walk of the Afterlife let out shouts of surprise. And then, when they saw Commander Berzerko coming fast behind him, they ran to hide.

It wasn't until he reached the Swamp of Swallowed Souls that Somber Kitty slowed down, realizing that he could not outfloat his pursuer.

"Meay." He looked behind him. For the moment the commander was out of sight. A noise behind Kitty made him turn. The swamp bubbled and howled, and many of the bubbles were shaped like Black Shuck dogs. They seemed to claw toward him, trying to pull him in.

Panting, he turned. He could hear Commander Berzerko coming down the corridor. He could hear the *tap, tap, tap* of her claws.

She came slowly. Clearly, she knew that Somber Kitty had reached a dead end.

May closed her eyes for the thirtieth time.

"Just concentrate on being over here instead of over there. It's easy."

"I'm trying," May said.

Lucius stood outside of the bars, looking in at her. He had asported in and out of the dungeon about twenty times, showing off.

"It's not really that easy," May said, frustrated. She tried to picture herself in the hallway beyond the bars where Lucius stood. She closed her eyes, then opened them. Again, she was still in the same place. "I just don't think it'll work for me, Lucius."

"It will. Just forget where you are. You have to *believe* you're here and not there."

May concentrated again. She could picture herself standing next to Lucius, outside the dungeon. She tried to believe it. She kept trying.

And suddenly, a very empty feeling came upon her. May mistook it for disappointment and opened her eyes. When she did, she let out a scream. Standing next to Lucius was . . . herself. At least, a version of herself. The girl looked like May, but she was as drifty and translucent as Lucius, and she was levitating about five feet from May.

Lucius studied the drifty spirit beside him and then studied the flesh-and-blood May Bird still standing inside the cell with her heart pounding.

"Oh, I guess it *is* impossible. You sent only your soul out."

May opened her mouth several times before she got out a reply. "Well, what do I do if my soul's out there and I'm in here?!" she asked, panicked.

The three stood there for a moment—Lucius, May, and May's soul—staring at one another helplessly. "Why don't you try closing your eyes again and getting her back?" Lucius suggested.

May did. She tried and tried, but every time she opened her eyes, her soul was still standing out in the corridor, staring at her forlornly. "I guess she can't get back through the bars," Lucius offered. "She doesn't seem very talkative, either."

"I suppose I'll just be going now," Lucius said with a sigh. Then, at May's look of shock, he giggled. "A joke! You don't think I'd leave you in there without your soul, do you?" He turned to May's soul. "I'm going to go look for a key."

Lucius zipped away in a ball of light. While he was gone, May and her soul stared at each other nervously. May thought about trying to make conversation, but she wasn't sure about what to say.

Several minutes went by before Lucius came zipping back, dangling a key in his hand. "*That* was easy," he said, looking dazed. "Very odd. The ghouls weren't even at their posts."

He felt around the invisible bars, zapping himself several times. May and her soul both winced sympathetically. Finally, he got it. "There!"

With a *click!* and a *snap!* and the sound of a door sliding open, May looked at the empty space, gingerly stepped toward it, and tiptoed across the threshold. There was no *zap*. No nothing. And a moment later she was standing beside her soul. The two reached out to touch each other's hands, and a blinding white light suddenly forced May to close her eyes. The emptiness inside went away as quickly as it had come, and her eyes fluttered open.

Lucius's grin infected her, and she smiled widely.

"Let's go find my cat," May said, turning businesslike.

Ding! Ding!

The floor beneath both of them shook. "What's that?" May asked. It sounded like the chimes of a giant clock.

Lucius looked up toward where the sound was coming from. "The big clock. It's nothing."

They zipped off down the hallway.

Chapter Thirty

A Sack of Dust

*D*eep in the woods of Briery Swamp, Ellen Bird was no longer charmed by what she saw in the lake. The swimmer beneath its surface had begun to stretch into eight glowing points. Her smile had widened to reveal a malicious grin.

An arrow of fear raced down Ellen's spine. The creature, now horrible instead of beautiful, reached toward her. . . .

And then it stopped.

As quickly as it had come, it turned and swam in the other direction, down, down, down, until it was only a point of light, and then the light went out.

May's mother turned for the woods and ran home.

Far above, all over the star known as the Ever After, Dark Spirits left their posts. Goblins and ghouls swarmed out of the villages toward the sea. Mummies and zombies ambled along side by side in the direction of the water. Every mean and twisted soul in the realm converged on South Place for the largest meeting of evil in the history of the Afterlife.

• • •

In Hocus Pocus, Pumpkin, Fabbio, and Bea had made it to the city limits before deciding to entrust Isabella to the others and try to follow after May Bird. Aghast, they watched from a sewer grate as Dark Spirits great and small clambered to the edges of the sea and leaped in.

"This is bad," Bea observed.

In fact, though nobody said it, they were all thinking the same thing: It was beginning to look as if the Lady had led May into a trap.

Above May and Lucius, the ceiling rocked with loud thuds. They both looked upward ominously, then at each other, then hurried on ahead, looking this way and that for Somber Kitty.

About ten minutes later they passed an arched opening onto a crumbling stone staircase that led downward.

"That's the Bogey's bedroom," Lucius said, turning dim.

May peered down the stairs, then up the hall. "Well," she said, biting her lip. "It could be that Kitty's already found his way there." She started down the stairs, then turned to Lucius. "You can stay here if you want. I'll be right back."

Lucius peered over his shoulder. "No thanks. I'll come with you."

They found the door at the end of the hall. It protruded from the wall in the shape of a dog's snout, two stone fangs jutting from the jowls and a knocker hanging from the great stone nose.

May hesitated a moment, looked at Lucius, then pushed on the nose. The door creaked open. She drifted inside, followed by Lucius.

The room was decorated in black and gold. An enormous

bed covered in a black velvet blanket dominated the space, the headboard carved with fearful faces. Stuffed animals—nine little Black Shuck dogs in all—were scattered across the pillows. There was a closet door and a black bureau next to it with gold, skull-shaped knobs. On top were several knickknacks— trophies for Realm's Deadliest Henchman, the Scariest Spirit Award, and several South Place Dance-Off ribbons, including one for Realm's Baddest Break-Dancer.

May looked at all these things in awe as Lucius hovered by the door. Her heart thrummed.

"Oh . . ."

"What?" May looked at Lucius, who had turned pale.

"Someone's coming."

Lucius grabbed the back of her shroud and yanked her down, shimmying both of them under the bed. They lay there, sick with fear.

A moment later a pair of feet drifted into the room. Another moment later two knees in black trousers appeared as the figure knelt on the floor. One unmistakable, horrifying suction-cup-tipped hand swept a wide arc under the bed. Back and forth. May pressed back, the fingertips within inches of her. She grabbed Lucius's hand, her own sweaty and trembling. And then the horrible fingers closed around something near her feet: a white, shiny piece of fabric.

The Bogey's hand disappeared, and he stood up. Then there was a rustle as the fabric was unfolded. From under the bed, it looked like a sequined, bell-bottom jumpsuit. While May watched in horror, the Bogey changed into the jumpsuit. And then he drifted out of the room.

After a few seconds passed, May tapped Lucius's back. "He's gone."

They peered out at the door for a moment longer, wanting to make sure. "In that outfit he really looked like a *boogie* man," May finally whispered.

"There must be a trapdoor or something," Lucius replied. May realized with a start that they were under the bed, right where she had been trying to get to all along.

"You're right!" She pivoted around on her belly and started searching the floor, coughing at the dust bunnies.

They felt all over the floor with their hands. Nothing. There was only one other thing underneath the bed, tucked back in the far corner—a tiny sack of some sort. May ignored it, feeling frantically along the ground. Finally, she and Lucius crawled out from under the bed and stared at each other.

Reconsidering, Lucius ducked back under and pulled out the little sack. They both looked down at it. May's heart fell into her feet.

FOR MAY BIRD, the tag said.

Glowing on the bag itself was a stamped label: SACK-O'-STARDUST.

May read the fine print under the stamp: *This Sack-O'-Stardust handcrafted by the spirits of North Farm. Good for inducing sneezes, putting out fires, and not much else.*

She raised her eyes, pale as Lucius. "What does it mean?"

Lucius opened the sack. "There's a note in here," he said, pulling it out and handing it to her.

May stood with her back to the Bogey's closet and slowly unfolded the paper. What it said made her blood run cold.

> May,
>> Home is behind you now.
>>> Sincerely,
>>> The Lady

May grabbed the sack from Lucius's hand and looked into it. "Dust," she whispered. "It's just dust." Was this a prank? A joke? May squatted and looked under the bed again—but there was nothing there.

May's body heated like a flame.

"The Lady of North Farm . . . ," Lucius mused. "I hear she's very tricky." He looked at May sympathetically. "I suppose it was all rumors after all."

"But she said . . ." May thought back to many things the Lady had said. And what she kept coming back to was this: that she was good, but also partly evil.

"Did you do something to make her mad?" Lucius asked.

May's head was spinning wildly. She couldn't speak or even think. She had relied on the Lady. She had counted on the Lady.

She had been wrong.

May clenched her fists, her eyes filling with tears. "What do I do?" Helplessly, she peered at herself in the Bogey's mirror.

The anger boiled inside her like lava. She waited for the tears to creep back under her eyelids, and then, with one shuddering breath, she pulled her bow from her back and headed for the door.

"Where are you going?"

May turned to Lucius. "To get what belongs to me."

As she floated out the door, Lucius zipped after her in awe. "Wait!"

May swiveled on him, her eyes flashing. "I'm not going to let things happen to me—to *us*—anymore. I'm going to *make* them happen." Her mouth straightened into a determined line. "I'm going to start with the Bogey. I'm going to make him tell me where my cat is."

She turned away quickly and strode ahead.

"You've gone mad!" Lucius yelled behind her, trying to keep up.

And he was right. May was so mad, she could hardly see.

In fact, floating down the hall, her bow in hand, the super-novas on her bathing suit exploding, her black hair flying, she was the very picture of a warrior.

Commander Berzerko turned the corner into the cavern of the Swallowed Souls, meeting her prey's eyes, her canines poking out of her jowls in a crocodile-like smile.

Somber Kitty, his back to the swamp, panted, his tongue hanging out of his mouth in an unsightly, embarrassing manner. His tail stood straight up. He swiped out with one tired paw, but caught nothing but air. "Meay." His knees gave way.

The commander, letting out a thin, satisfied hiss, took a step closer. And then she floated into the air, puffing out. Her fur became spiky, smoke poured from her ears. Somber Kitty wiggled his nose, sniffing the air. He tilted his head to the left and the right.

"Mew," he said curiously.

And then Commander Berzerko's tail lashed out toward him.

At that moment Kitty's fatigue, which he of course had been faking, disappeared. With astounding energy, he leaped sideways, dodging the tail gracefully.

And then Somber Kitty did what any cat who knew martial arts would do. He gave Commander Berzerko a swift karate chop. The commander careened against a nearby wall and bounced back, howling.

As she flew by him, Somber Kitty leaped into the air and executed a lightning-fast judo kick, sending the commander flying across the cavern like an air hockey puck. The commander let out a mew of surprise as she sailed right into the swamp.

She scrambled against the edges of the bubbly ooze, letting out a long screech. But the bubbles, barking and snarling, dragged her down.

One outstretched paw remained above the swamp's churning surface for a moment longer, and then it, too, sank out of sight.

Nothing remained of Commander Berzerko but a small and sparkling object lying on the shore.

Somber Kitty sniffed the glistening diamond collar with disdain, then hurried away.

Chapter Thirty-one

The Dastardly Disco

It had been an agonizing few minutes for Beatrice, Pumpkin, and Fabbio. They just didn't know what to do. Hurry into the lighthouse and head after May Bird, which also meant heading into pretty certain doom? Or stay where they were, which would leave their friend in danger? Nobody, of course, considered choosing the second option. But they couldn't quite figure out how to tackle the first.

"I don't know how, but I'm going after her," Pumpkin finally said, pushing up against the sewer grate as Bea held him back.

"Pumpkin, wait!" She grabbed the bottom of his trousers, but Pumpkin kept floating forward, until—holding on with all her might—Bea flopped out onto the street in a heap.

Fabbio leaped out of the sewer and tried to pull her back by her feet. "We are just . . . needing to . . . think of a plan, Punkin."

It was as they were pulling Beatrice like a jump rope when they noticed a pair of familiar slitted green eyes staring at them through the lighthouse doorway.

Beckoning.

• • •

The Bogey, whom May and Lucius had caught up with a mere two halls away from his room, drifted on ahead, and May drifted along behind him, Lucius tugging on her shroud from time to time and making an *Are you crazy?* face.

"You don't have to come," she whispered over her shoulder, never taking her eyes off the Bogey's back.

They floated all the way up to the first floor of South Place behind him, then twisted through a maze of hallways.

Soon they came to a pair of double doors at the end of a hall. The Bogey paused, straightened his white bell-bottom jumpsuit, adjusted his top hat so it sat just so, and pushed through the doors and through a thick curtain.

May and Lucius slipped in after him, peering out from behind the curtain as the doors closed behind them. They were in a dark room sparkling with purple strobe lights crisscrossing the floor. Somewhere far above, someone coughed.

"And now, introducing your host . . ."

May stood up straight, pulled an arrow from her back, and aimed.

From all around, a thrumming beat began. From above, a spotlight focused on the Bogey.

". . . the Bogey!"

And then the world seemed to come to a halt.

May's heart froze within her as her eyes drifted upward to take in an enormous hall—nine stories high, layered with hundreds of jagged balconies piling one on top of the other to the ceiling. And each one was teeming—*teeming*—with ghouls, goblins, zombies, trolls, mummies, and every other dark thing that had ever roamed the realm. There were so many tiers extending so far up that May couldn't even see beyond them.

An enormous clock ran up one side of the vast hall, with an equally enormous golden pendulum, and draped across it was a banner lit by a spotlight:

REALM TAKEOVER KICKOFF PARTY

The strobe lights flickered across the masses that were clinging to the balconies like countless germs. Their teeth were large, their claws sharp, and their faces were set with malice.

The first beats of a song began to pound over loudspeakers all over the walls, shaking the floor. May and Lucius shrank back against the door. In the middle of the floor the Bogey thrust his arms upward in a dramatic maneuver. And then he began to dance.

The Dastardly Disco had begun.

Chapter Thirty-two

Somber Kitty Dances at Midnight

South Place appeared to be deserted. But Fabbio, Bea, Pumpkin, and Kitty knew better.

"Where is everyone?" Beatrice asked. With no one to hide from, they were winding down the spiral of the realm in a fraction of the time it had taken May and Kitty.

"I have very bad feeling no words can describe," Fabbio offered. "Which is not usual for me," he added in a whisper.

Ignoring their gut instincts, which told them to escape while they still could, they followed Somber Kitty farther and farther downward.

Up ahead, they could hear the sound of impossibly loud music.

As May and Lucius watched from the cover of the curtains, the ghouls and goblins and zombies poured down from the balconies—climbing, scrabbling, practically dripping from the tiers above to join the Bogey on the dance floor.

> *Blame it on the sunshine,*
> *Blame it on the moonlight,*

> *Blame it on the good times,*
> *Blame it on the boogie . . .*

Everywhere, they fell into the same steps as the Bogey: *Step, step, growl. Step, step, growl, lurch.*

It was the world's most terrifying line dance.

Back and forth, around and around, the Dark Spirits jerked and slithered.

For the length of the song, the Dark Spirits did their dance, and the two friends behind the curtain looked on in awe. When the music finally stopped, a microphone descended from somewhere far above, landing in the middle of the floor, where the Bogey scooped it up. The clock marked the time: 11:56.

"In a few minutes the guest of honor will be arriving."

The Dark Spirits scrambled back up to their seats, snarling and stomping as they arrived in their rows, until only the Bogey was left on the floor.

"He's taken a trip down from his fortress to make a special announcement," the Bogey continued. "So special that you've all been excused from your haunting duties for the night." More snarling and stomping. "At the stroke of midnight he'll be arriving. . . ."

The music leaped to life again. Everyone peered at the clock. It was 11:57. Every head turned in the direction of the ninth-floor balcony, which was completely empty. May, too, stared at the empty balcony. She knew, of course, who would be appearing there. Her fear had turned into a ribbon inside her, tying her to the place where she stood.

Lucius took hold of the back of her shroud and whispered in her ear, "We've got to get out of here."

• • •

Far down at the end of the hall Somber Kitty saw a pair of double doors. He sniffed the air, then turned back to the others.

"Meay," he said very surely, and zipped ahead.

The others hurried after him.

May let Lucius pull her backward, toward the doors. One step. Two steps.

Thwap!

As the doors behind them burst open, they went hurtling forward, sailing through the slit in the curtains and sliding onto the dance floor. Pumpkin, then Beatrice and Fabbio, came sprawling after them. Only Somber Kitty stayed on all fours. The group landed in a tight knot, in full view of all the spectators.

The hall went completely quiet.

For a moment no one knew what to do. May pulled her death shroud tightly around herself as she and her friends stood slowly, peering about the hall. The Bogey was frozen in place, his white eyeballs glinting at them. Even the thousands upon thousands of Dark Spirits were still as statues.

Someone had forgotten to stop the music. The speakers started blaring out the next tune.

> *Well, you can tell by the way I use my walk*
> *I'm a woman's man, no time to talk . . .*

And then, finally, one creature moved.

As May and the others looked on, Somber Kitty stood on his hind legs and began to dance.

Chapter Thirty-three

The Guest of Honor

"Utt are you *ooing*?" Pumpkin whispered, trying not to move his lips as he smiled broadly into the balconies, making like he was enjoying the disco.

Somber Kitty ignored him, executed a twirl, a swivel hip, and his favorite, a fouetté, keeping perfect time with the rhythm of the music.

> *Ah, ha, ha,*
> *Stayin' alive, stayin' alive*

May and the others watched with wide eyes, and then May looked up at the faces of the Dark Spirits. They were nudging one another curiously and pointing to the graceful creature on the floor, who was not only a cat, but a *dancing* cat.

"He's trying to confuse them," she whispered. And it looked to be working. At least for the moment.

The Dark Spirits started cheering. May and the others fake smiled at one another. They all began to move awkwardly. Fabbio thrust one finger into the air and rocked his hips stiffly. Beatrice swayed elegantly. Pumpkin executed "the worm," a break-dance move he'd seen on TV while haunting White Moss Manor. Together, they all danced backward toward the double doors.

Ding, ding, ding, ding!

As the great clock struck midnight, lightning bolts snaked their way across the dark ceiling of the room, smoke billowing out above them. The music stopped. All eyes turned to the uppermost balcony, where a dark silhouette had emerged. The figure wore a wide-brimmed hat pulled down over his eyes and an old, worn jacket.

The hall shook, as if with an earthquake, sending spirits toppling all over the place and the small knot of dancers on the floor sprawling.

Pumpkin scrambled behind May. Fabbio reached for Beatrice. Somber Kitty leaped in front of them all and growled.

"Hello." The dark figure's voice echoed against the walls and reverberated loudly around the hall. Though he was far, far above, May could feel his eyes resting on her. "May Bird, is it?" Bo Cleevil shook his head carelessly. "You look very familiar, little speck."

With a wave of his hand, a great wind gusted through the hall, blowing May's death shroud back so that it clung to her neck by its strap just barely. She clasped the neck strap with both hands and held on tight.

"Let's see . . . Here's a fact I heard recently . . . 'Known far and wide as the girl who destroyed evil Bo Cleevil's reign of terror. Resides in Briery Swamp, West Virginia,'" Bo Cleevil quoted from *The Book of the Dead*.

The Bogey let out a raspy whimper, and the Dark Spirits shifted and murmured.

"I was told you'd been made into nothing." Bo Cleevil tapped his chin thoughtfully. "Let me think. Who told me that? Ah, yes."

He thrust out a finger and pointed at the Bogey. "Bogey, you've been bad."

Before the Bogey could so much as tremble, a shaft of light shot from Bo Cleevil's finger.

The smoke cleared a moment later—and all that was left of the Bogey was a top hat and a pile of ash.

You could have heard a pin drop in the great hall.

Bo Cleevil went on, sounding perfectly relaxed. "I'm glad you could make it to our party, May. You see, this is where the Ever After as we all know it ends."

He swept the crowd with his eyes. "As you know, I have an announcement. After tonight there will be no more South Place."

The Dark Spirits whispered and jabbered.

"No more realm under the sea for you. It's dark. It's messy. Forget it. Tonight we're leaving it behind. We're moving upstairs. Permanently."

The spirits in the balconies let out dreadful cheers as Bo Cleevil turned his attention back to May and, with a gesture, indicated they should quiet down.

"I'm curious to hear how you've found your way this far, little speck. But more lazy, really, than curious."

He thrust out a finger again, and the air beneath May's feet began to vibrate and change. Suddenly, May was being lifted into the air.

She soared up, up, up, until she was a hundred feet or more

above the dance floor, looking down on her friends and level with Bo Cleevil.

Desperately, she fumbled behind her back and pulled out her bow, slipping an arrow into the notch. She took aim.

Bo Cleevil laughed and waggled one finger, sending the arrow plummeting to the ground with a tidy *plunk*. May was pulled through the air toward him until she was hovering right above the rail of his tier, just inches from him, still clutching her bow.

Bo Cleevil studied her. His eyes gleamed like coals from underneath the shadow of his hat, and in them May saw everything she feared: coldness, hatred. And something else: emptiness.

Even more than being scared, May felt the loneliest she had ever felt. She tried to squirm, but she could not move her arms or legs an inch. She looked down at her friends. And then she thought of what the note under the Bogey's bed had said: *Home is behind you now.* It was coming true.

She couldn't believe it. She didn't want to believe it. And then . . .

"Oh," May groaned.

In a flash she could see it: standing in the Bogey's room, reading the note. She remembered just where she'd been standing when she'd read it.

Home is behind *you now.*

The Lady *was* tricky.

The Bogey's portal wasn't under his bed.

When she had read the Lady's note, May had been standing with her back to the Bogey's closet.

Chapter Thirty-four

Dust in the Wind

With a simple flick of his index finger, Bo Cleevil sent May whipping around in the air until she was upside down, just above his head.

He laughed and flicked his finger again. May shook like a leaf. The rest of her arrows clattered to the ground, leaving only her bow, which she just managed to strap to her back. Other things fell out of her pockets: a Ghouly Gum wrapper Pumpkin had stuffed in there; a rubber band from the Colony of the Undead; a feather from the night they had dressed up at Risk Falls.

Bo Cleevil shook her again, for good measure. As May tilted this way and that, the Sack-o'-Stardust in her pocket, which she hadn't closed, shook out its contents.

The last speck of dust fluttered out of the sack. It trickled through the air, crossing the distance between May's pocket and Bo Cleevil's face. It drifted, quietly and unseen, into his left eye.

As May watched in confusion, Bo Cleevil winced, and his eye began to water. And then he wrinkled his nose and sneezed.

May went plummeting downward.

She was just a few feet above the ground when Cleevil recovered himself and thrust out his arm, drawing her back up. But May felt a sudden new weight on her feet.

Fabbio was hanging on to her ankles for dear life.

May slipped an inch downward. At the same time the pull from above got stronger, and she began to rise again, Fabbio still dangling beneath her.

"No!"

Below, Beatrice leaped at Fabbio's feet, tripping over her dress but managing to grab on. Again, May sank . . . and rose. Beatrice's feet left the ground.

Lucius jumped next, tackling Bea around the knees. Down and then up they went. Down on the ground, Pumpkin looked back at Somber Kitty, bit his fingers, and lunged for Lucius. Somber Kitty came last of all. He hurled himself at Pumpkin's toes and dug his front claws into the bottom of Pumpkin's trousers. His back claws dug into the floor.

It was as if Bo Cleevil and Somber Kitty were having a great tug-of-war. While Cleevil pulled with a force no one could see, Somber Kitty pulled with his toes, and all of May's friends pulled with him.

As if they were all in an immense vacuum, things started flying about all over the dance hall—tiaras, pitchforks, whips, chains, pocketbooks. May's shroud pulled upward on her neck, sucked by the wind Bo Cleevil had created. With one hand, she untied it, and it went flying into Bo Cleevil's face.

Amid the din, the Dark Spirits gabbled in awe. May was resplendent, wildly alive. The supernovas on her bathing suit continued to explode, and her dark hair flew behind her. Her eyes searched the room for a way to escape. And then she saw it, beneath her.

"I need that arrow!" she hollered to Fabbio, pointing with her chin to the place on the floor where the first fallen one had landed, now near Kitty's feet.

"May needs a that arrow," Fabbio called into the whirlwind, to Beatrice, who called to Lucius, who called to Pumpkin. Pumpkin, still desperately holding on to Lucius's ankle with one hand, swooped the other long arm down around Kitty, who was still dug in on Pumpkin's pants, and managed to grab the arrow and pass it upward.

A moment later May had it in her hands.

May pulled her bow from her back and took aim. She took a deep breath, focused her eye on the spot she intended to hit, and let the arrow fly.

The shot went straight into the palm of Bo Cleevil's hand. The hand trembled for an instant, then went silver. A shriek shook the walls of the hall as he stumbled backward.

May and the others fell again, this time all the way to the floor below, landing in a smushy heap.

As they yanked one another upright, Lucius gushed, "Not *bad*!" His blue eyes were wide and admiring. All around them, the Dark Spirits stared, flabbergasted.

May retrieved her death shroud from where it had fluttered to the floor and retied it around her neck.

Then, right as she looked up, the Dark Spirits let out howls of rage and started clambering down from the balconies.

Chapter Thirty-five

The Bogey's Closet

The entire hall shook as Bo Cleevil continued to howl. A balcony above buckled. A gaggle of snarling goblins blocked the doors.

"This way!" Beatrice said, leading the group in the other direction. Suddenly, a troop of zombies leaped from the first tier and landed in front of them.

May and the others stood poised in the middle. The two groups of Dark Spirits closed in toward each other. May and her friends gathered into a tight knot, backing up.

The goblins directed at the zombies a collective *"Grrrrr,"* which was goblin for "Have you ever seen anything more tacky?"

The zombies directed at the goblins a collective *"Eeeuuughhhh,"* which of course meant only "Eeeuuughhhh."

And then, all the years of animosity between the two groups finally exploding, the zombies and the goblins hurled themselves at each other, ignoring the fugitives completely.

May looked at Beatrice, and Beatrice gave her the same bewildered look back. Then they all zipped toward the doors, and this time passed safely through them. Bo Cleevil let out another, hall-shaking howl of rage, and behind them the frame of the door came tumbling down.

As they sprinted into the corridor, the walls around them shook, as if South Place was undergoing an earthquake.

"Ohhhhh," Pumpkin moaned.

As they turned the corner, a voice resounded through the hallway, and the force of it blew them like a wind. It was Bo Cleevil's voice, and it seemed to come from each and every particle of air around them. "MAY BIRD!" it screamed.

"Let's go, let's go!" Lucius ushered everyone forward. May brought up the rear, carrying Somber Kitty against her ribs. They zipped down the hall that led to the Bogey's bedroom, scurrying in the direction of the entrance to the Lazy Way Ladder that Lucius had pointed out earlier. But at the top of the Bogey's stairs, May paused.

Pumpkin, zipping up ahead, turned back to look for her, then stopped short. The others did the same. Everybody was wondering the same thing: Why had May stopped?

"The way out for me is down there," she said, staring at them earnestly. "I think." She glanced down a flight of stairs that would take her to the Bogey's bedroom. She didn't just think. "I *know*."

Behind them, something enormous slammed, and they heard the grunts of hundreds of Dark Spirits in pursuit. But none of the friends moved. Pumpkin looked stricken.

"Well, what are you waiting for!" Beatrice cried.

May shook her head unsurely. "I don't know if I can leave you."

"This your wish," Fabbio said. "This why you come so far, little May. You must go."

"Meow." Somber Kitty twisted around and gave her a serious look. Their mother needed them too.

Jabbers and growls and snarls were coming from all directions now as the Dark Spirits wound their way along various routes.

May scanned her friends. "But how will you get out?"

"It's not a problem," Lucius said. "Trust me."

Bea's eyes filled with tears. "We'll be fine." She wrapped her arms around May's neck and gave her a tight hug. "We won't give you a choice. There's no time for long good-byes. Go!"

Fabbio hugged May next and then kissed Somber Kitty on the top of the head. Then Lucius gave May an awkward embrace and rubbed Kitty's ears. When he pulled back, May stood hesitating on the brink of the stairs. Only Pumpkin was left. He was leaning against the opposite wall, pretending not to see her.

"Pumpkin?"

"You gotta go," he said, looking down at his fingers. "I know. I always knew you would."

Finally, he looked at her, his big black eyes wide and sorrowful.

"Oh, Pumpkin—"

Just as May took a step toward him, there was a crash. A gang of ghouls filled the end of the hall behind them.

May and her friends took one last look at each other as Fabbio grabbed Pumpkin's shirt, and Lucius spirited the group forward in the direction of the ladder. One by one, they disappeared, Pumpkin last of all.

The last sight May had of him was his sad face under his

waving tuft of hair and then his long fingers, reaching out toward her for a hug that would never happen now, before they disappeared around the bend.

May took in a shuddering breath. And then, with Kitty in her arms, she turned and zoomed down the stairs.

Within minutes, May was standing in front of the Bogey's closet. She sent up a silent wish to a million stars before grabbing the door handle and yanking it open. She and Kitty stood there, looking in, wide-eyed and stunned.

Amid the boxes of shoes and row upon row of black suits was a puddle in the middle of the floor. But it wasn't like any puddle May had ever seen. It made an enormous sucking sound and gaped at her. Small lights, like tiny stars, twinkled in its depths.

Next to it a tiny wheel caught her eye. It had a small arrow mounted on a spinner in the middle, and the arrow could point to one of four different-colored sections of a map of Earth. Tiny stars marked the four portals in the four corners of the globe. May drew a finger to her lips and then very gently, very carefully, took the arrow and pointed it to the star that marked Briery Swamp.

Now all that was left, she guessed, was to leap.

May hesitated. She looked back at the door to the Bogey's bedroom. Beyond it lay her worst fears: the goblins, ghouls, Bo Cleevil. But also beyond it were her friends—and a place in the universe that claimed to need her.

Need her.

May looked at the pool on the floor of the closet again.

Underneath it was her mom and everything that was warm and as comfy as a fuzzy mitten. Underneath it was home.

May peered into the watery blackness.

"I can't, Kitty. I can't leave them."

Turning, she rushed back to the bedroom door and quickly turned the corner—into a hallway packed with ghouls coming toward her.

Clutching Somber Kitty tightly, May backed into the bedroom again, looking around for a place to hide, a different way to escape.

She looked to the closet again, knowing there was no other way.

She crept to the edge of the puddle. She closed her eyes and counted to three. And then she turned to look over her shoulder. The first of the ghouls had gained on the doorway and were lunging toward her.

May hoped for luck . . . and leaped.

Chapter Thirty-six

Under the Night

The sky was dark above but for the occasional flash of lightning flickering on raindrops as they plummeted toward the tiny lake far below.

The moon, hidden by the storm clouds, had no view. And so she missed it when a little girl burst out from the surface of the lake and scrambled up on shore, pulling herself across the dirt and finally resting a few feet from the water's edge, as soppy and bedraggled as a wet mouse.

May pulled Kitty out of her shroud. She filled her lungs deeply with air and continued lying on her back, looking up in space.

Had she made it? Had she really made it?

May sat up, then stood on shaky legs and turned to take in the trees, the briars, the sky. There were no zipping stars in it, no gray dusk hanging.

It was *night*.

May took another deep breath. And then she laughed. She held out her arms and flung her head back and howled. She hopped from foot to foot, Somber Kitty watching from a safe distance, slightly embarrassed for her.

Exhausted, her legs giving way beneath her, May sank back down to the ground, running her fingers happily into the soft mud, eyeing her bathing suit, which no longer glowed or sparkled. Her heart gave a hard ache, and she ran her hands over the fabric, then looked back up in the sky.

She ran through the briars like the prickers didn't matter. She needed to know that she was really here, and she wouldn't believe it for real until she she saw it: White Moss Manor.

Home.

Bursting onto the front lawn, she took in the sight. Every light in the house was on, as they had been—though May didn't know it—ever since she'd disappeared. She took a step toward the house, began to run, and then she stopped right there in the middle of the grass and looked into the sky one more time.

Somewhere, someone needed her. Somewhere, they thought she was a hero.

She leveled her eyesight back on the house and spied a face in the window. A worried face under brown curls. It hadn't seen her yet.

May ran for the porch, Somber Kitty tucked in her arms, taking the steps two at a time. She stopped short of the door and her stomach did a flop. A tiny white envelope was waiting for her there on the brushy welcome mat. Seeing the familiar stamp, she picked it up and slit it open, pulling out the letter in a flash.

> *Dearest May,*
>   *Congratulations. I knew you could do it. You see, I*
> *am not all that bad.*

She kept reading.

> Don't forget about the stardust. Don't forget about
> the quartz rocks in the woods. You are small. But you
> are also so much more.

May smiled, her lips bunching up as she tried not to cry.

> And don't forget, we still need you.
> Don't forget us.
>> Sincerely,
>> The Lady of North Farm

The letter began to shrivel, then turned to dust in May's fingers. It fell through the cracks between them and then through the cracks in the porch beneath her feet.

May looked at her front door, taking one final deep breath. She turned the knob.

"Mom!" she called as she gave a big push and burst inside. She left the door open behind her.

Out on the lawn, only a spider and a ladybug heard the muffled sound of pounding feet running down the stairs and the happy cries of two people who loved each other very much saying hello after a long good-bye.

The trees missed it completely. Right then their attention was turned in another direction, upward, toward a star that was growing dim.